Perfect Timing

Patsy Collins

ISBN- 978-1-914339-30-1

Contents

1. On Time

"I'll just go and change the setting on the alarm, otherwise I might forget about it tonight," Davie McGregor told his wife.

"Are you putting it forward or back?" Alison asked.

"I'll set it to six fifteen."

"Six fifteen! Do we really have to get up so early, Davie?"

"I'm afraid I do. Now I'm manager I'll have to be first in. It's a matter of honour. I shouldn't expect my staff to work longer hours than me."

"No, I suppose not," Alison agreed as she began making their supper.

"If you'd rather, I could put my clothes ready in the bathroom. If I got up quietly you could sleep in a bit later, Alison love."

"No, I'll get up with you. Anyway, that wouldn't help much would it? If we don't get a lift in with you, we'd have to get the bus and that would mean leaving just as early."

Alison sighed; she would have to wake her son early now so that he could share some time with his father. Davie was still hard at work when his son was being read a bedtime story. Davie always went straight up to say goodnight to him, but the boy was usually asleep. Alison wondered if the church nursery their son attended would take him earlier. She could ring Julia and ask, in fact as she glanced at the clock she decided that she must do so right away.

"I'm sorry to inconvenience you, but I need to re arrange my schedule a little. Would half an hour earlier be possible?" Alison explained why she wanted to change her son's hours. "As you know, my husband drives us in to town. He will be going in earlier from now on."

"Yes, I can manage that," Julia Grand reassured her. "Will you still collect him at the same time?"

She would have to of course. That meant more hours to be paid for. It was a good thing Davie had gained that promotion.

Teresa Roberts reluctantly altered the hands on the silver alarm clock, to ensure they would be woken a little earlier than had previously been the case.

"Six ten. Douglas, must we get up quite so early?" Mrs Roberts asked her husband.

"Well I must, darling. I know I now have a new manager, but I do still own the company. I really ought to be first to arrive. Setting a good example, you know, keeping up the standards."

"I see your point. Six ten it is," his wife conceded.

"I'll try not to disturb you, Teresa, darling."

"Don't be silly, I shall get up to have breakfast with you and see you off to work. It's only proper."

Douglas Roberts smiled at his wife; she always knew the right thing to do.

"Thank you, darling. I hope it will not be an inconvenience?"

"Not at all. There are plenty of things for me to do, both

here and in the village. Getting an early start will be a positive advantage. Now, what would you like for breakfast? If you fancy porridge, I shall put it to soak otherwise there are kippers or scrambled eggs."

Douglas's smile broadened. He hadn't much fancied making do with the piece of toast he would have prepared for himself, if his wife had wished to sleep in.

"Mum, can I borrow your alarm?" Sue Wilson asked as she emerged, wrapped in towels, from the bathroom.

"Early start, lass?" her mother asked, handing over the pink, flower shaped clock.

"From now on it will be. Since Davie McGregor became manager, he's started coming in early. As his secretary, I should be there ready to start as soon as he arrives. It's a matter of principle."

Sue's mother was pleased her daughter took her job seriously, but a little sad too. These early starts meant equally early nights. Sue would not now be able to attend the remaining confirmation classes which were held after evensong every Tuesday.

"Well don't you go overdoing it, love. There's more to life than work you know."

"I know, Mum. They're good to me really, that's why I don't want to let them down. Anyway, I'm sure Reverend Grand will understand. He's keen on hard work. Perhaps he'll be able to see me at a different time?"

"Perhaps so. You're right about him thinking hard work's a good thing any road."

"Morning, Burt, you're up early, not after my job are you?"

the milkman called to his neighbour.

"No mate, I'm still cleaning up at Roberts and Co. They've all started coming in early. It's a job to get everything done before they arrive."

"Still you'll finish early won't you? Swings and roundabouts mate. Swings and roundabouts," the milkman said. He waved, and was gone.

Burt didn't mind getting up early, but he did mind leaving his wife alone. Her health, never good, has deteriorated recently. She was now unable to get out of bed unaided. Burt usually helped her up and into the bathroom. He ensured she was warm and comfortable, with a book within reach, before going to work. Her carer arrived an hour later and stayed until he was home. The arrangement had been working well. Now his wife would either sit alone for almost two hours, waiting to be washed and dressed, or she would have to stay in bed. Burt and his wife would have to talk to the carer and see what she advised. Perhaps that kind lady would alter her hours?

"Good morning Alison. Have you been waiting long?" Alison's manageress asked, as she arrived to open the store.

"Not long. Davie drops me on his way to work. He's just been promoted and he starts earlier now," Alison explained.

"Promoted eh? And an early start all round is one of the perks?"

"It seems that way."

"Well don't worry, love; I'll open up the shop a bit earlier."

"I don't want to put you to any trouble."

"Don't worry about it. I can't have you waiting out in the cold can I?"

"Good morning, Vicar, Mrs Roberts here," Teresa boomed into the telephone. "I wondered, would it be convenient for me to do the flowers earlier on Thursdays? We have changed our routine at home and I like to carry out my duties first thing."

"That should be fine," the vicar assured her. "I'll ask the verger to make certain he unlocks earlier and gets the heating switched on."

The vicar smiled as he replaced the handset. Finally, he had a fresh idea for his sermon; the virtues of rising early. Mrs Roberts was a refreshing change from those who slept in until the last possible moment and were then reluctant to carry out a proper day's work. He was thinking, unconsciously, of the slow progress of repairs to the rectory. The Monday following this sermon, several of his congregation set their alarms a little earlier than had previously been the case. Not the builders though.

Reverend Grand was puzzled by the builders. They were very thorough and, once they did arrive, very hard working. Their skill was undoubted. The bill was for the total job, not the hours worked, so the time taken was a small inconvenience rather than a real concern. Still he didn't understand and decided to ask to the foreman for an explanation.

"If you began earlier in the day you could complete more jobs, earn more money," he said.

"Surely, Vicar you're not suggesting I cultivate love of money over concern for my fellow man and personal fulfilment?"

The builder laughed at the vicar's puzzled expression and explained. He told him that he and his men all lived in the same small village. "When we leave with our vans, we hold the traffic up a fair bit. It's all narrow lanes, see? We didn't want to inconvenience our neighbours as a matter of principle, so we decided we could either leave before them, or after the morning rush. If we start early it's not just us, it's our families that are put out too. We wouldn't see our kids so much. We'd go to bed earlier, so we'd have less time with friends or for hobbies. We earn reasonable money, so we decided that we would start just a bit later."

The post was late again. Reverend Grand commented on this as he accepted a pile of letters from the postman.

"It's rather inconvenient; I often don't get time to go through them properly before I must begin dealing with parish matters."

"Sorry, Vicar, but it looks like this will be the regular time now. Traffic round here is getting much busier in the mornings. I'm never the only one about now, and so I get held up."

Reverend Grand remembered his sermon on early rising, and decided to refrain from further comment. His perusal of the letters was interrupted by the harsh ring of his telephone.

"Dad, I'm sorry, but I can't take that dog after all. I have to work longer hours in the nursery now and it just wouldn't be fair," Julia Grand told her father.

The vicar thought of Mr Roberts. He'd owned a dog years ago, he'd not had another because of business commitments. Perhaps now that he had taken on a new manager he would have the time?

Reverend Grand returned his attention to his letter; it was from Sue Wilson, to explain her absence from the confirmation classes. There was also a note from Burt, the cleaner at Roberts and Co, who wondered if the vicar knew of anyone who might be willing to sit with his wife for an hour or so, early in the mornings. He placed his mail into a reasonably tidy pile. Next, he called to the verger, "I won't be long, I'm just popping out to see a man about a dog."

"I would love to have a dog, Reverend, but I simply don't know if I'll have the time."

"Time seems to be a problem for everyone, but it's a more serious problem for this particular spaniel I'm afraid."

"What do you mean?"

"The shelter he's in is closing down. Most of the dogs have been found homes. My daughter was to take him, Rex his name is, but she's another one who doesn't have the time."

"Is there no one else who could take him?"

"Again it's an issue of time. All dogs have to be housed by the weekend, or …"

"A spaniel you say?"

"Yes, he's young and friendly. I'm sure you'll like him."

"Teresa love, in future you can sleep in," Douglas Roberts told his wife. "I'll bring you a cup of tea when I come back from walking the dog."

"Won't that make you late for work, darling?"

"I've decided it might be better if I went in slightly later. My staff are all hard working and conscientious, I can trust them, even when I'm not there. I saw Davie McGregor packing his wife and son into the car this morning, whilst I was out with Rex."

"He is the manager. Surely it's important for him to be on time?"

"On time is one thing, but this was before dawn. The whole family looked tired. Can't have my manager overworking like that. It's a matter of honour."

"So, what will you do?"

"I've done it already, my dear. I said as long as the work gets done, it really doesn't matter who arrives first. I've told him to put his alarm back a bit, not to come in until he's due to start. That should set a good example to the others."

Davie McGregor's family now eat a leisurely breakfast together, Sue has been confirmed, Rex has learned to sit and the builders have finished work; exactly on schedule.

2. Girls' Night Out

When I walked into The Frog and Bucket, the others were already at the bar; except Emma. After our conversation the day before, I'd hoped she'd have made an effort to be early.

"See you in The Frog and Bucket tomorrow?" I'd said.

"There again? Can't we just do something spontaneous?" Emma had asked.

"Like what?"

"I don't know. If we decide now, it won't be spontaneous, will it?"

"No, but if we leave it to you, we'll be spontaneously hanging about waiting until it's too late to go anywhere."

"Lou!"

"You know I'm right. So, see you Friday?"

She'd agreed and promised to be on time.

A glance at the clock showed it was just gone ten to eight, so to be fair, she wasn't late – yet.

"What are you having, Lou?" Cara said.

"Vodka and lime, please. Were you waiting for me?" I asked when I realised none of them had drinks.

"Yes, I saw your bus go by as I came in, so thought we might as well wait," Melanie said.

"We're not waiting for Emma, though," Tasha said. "I can't wait until she decides to put in an appearance."

The others agreed and made jokes about dying of thirst

and needing to be back at work on Monday.

"It's not really funny though," Cara said. "She should stick to The Plan, not just act as though it doesn't matter which night we meet."

"Yes and she knows I have trouble with transport, so it's not fair to keep changing locations," Melanie said.

I added that I liked to know what I was doing, not just leave everything to chance.

It's no secret that Emma isn't best known for her reliability. I don't mean she's not a good friend; she is. We can always trust her to offer sympathy for a broken heart, lend us her favourite dress or tell us honestly if the hairstyle we're considering would be a big mistake. What you can never expect from Emma is that she'll remember where she was supposed to meet or that she'll turn up on time or even the right day.

All of our group have, more than once, stood in the rain on a street corner waiting for her, or sat alone in a pub, or missed films or concerts because of Emma. That's why we developed The Friday Night Plan. It's a simple plan; we meet between seven thirty and eight (to allow for the buses) on the first Friday of the month (so it's easy to remember) in The Frog and Bucket (so we're warm, dry and have ready access to drinks).

I sat down with one of the conveniently available drinks and caught up on the gossip.

Cara had another new boyfriend, although that didn't mean she'd ditched the other two. "I have to be very organised to keep track of where I'm supposed to be and when and who with," she explained.

I didn't need to check my watch to know Emma hadn't

been organised enough to manage that tonight.

Tasha was considering going blonde and Melanie had got a job at last.

"I'll have to get up at six to get the bus, but I'm not worried about that; unlike some people I don't like to be late."

The pub's clock showed Emma was fifteen minutes late.

At half past eight, Tasha said, "Are we having another round here?"

I rang Emma. No answer.

"Perhaps that means she's driving and on her way here?" I said.

When we'd bitched and giggled our way through our second drinks, I rang Emma again. Still no answer.

"Do you think she's all right?" I asked.

"She's always all right," Tasha reminded me. "We always worry and she's always forgotten or got distracted or couldn't make it and didn't think to let us know."

"You're right," I agreed and headed for the bar.

I'd just started to give my order when the others came over.

"Let's not wait. I want to go to the club and if we leave it any longer we'll have trouble getting in," Tasha said.

"She's right," Cara agreed. "We can leave a message for Emma. It might teach her a lesson if we didn't though. She's got no excuse; she could have walked from Nial House by now."

"Terrible about that, isn't it?" the landlord said.

"What's terrible?" I asked.

"The fire at Nial House. All those people trapped and …

You didn't know?"

We all shook our heads.

"Our friend lives there and she hasn't turned up …"

"The pretty redhead? Look, I don't know all the details, but most of the people were evacuated."

"We'd better go round and check she's OK," Melanie said.

"Sorry, girls but you won't be able to do that. The whole area is cordoned off. Two of my bar staff were late because they had to go right out to Palmerston Road to get here."

Tasha said exactly what I was thinking, "There must be something we can do."

"Your best bet is to keep out the way and let the firemen do their job. You said your mate was going to join you tonight?"

We nodded.

"So she'll know where to find you if she needs help."

That made sense, so we ordered soft drinks and prepared to wait. The landlord promised to let us know if he heard anything else.

"She'll be all right, Lou," Cara said.

The pub door opened and we turned to look. It wasn't Emma.

"If she'd got out, she'd be here wouldn't she? Or she'd have answered her phone at least," I said. "She never turns her phone off."

"That's true. She knows she's sometimes late and makes sure people can get hold of her," Melanie agreed.

"It's not just that. She has it on all night and answers no matter what time it is," Tasha said. "I rang her once when I was upset and then apologised when I saw how late it was.

She said it was never too late to help a friend …" She had to stop and blow her nose. "Three in the morning it was and she offered to come round and make me toast and cocoa, and tonight I wouldn't even wait an hour so she could come clubbing with us."

The pub was filling fast. Every time the door opened we hoped Emma would come through it.

She didn't.

"I gave her a lecture yesterday about always being late," I told them. "I forgot it's not always her fault. Remember when I tried to colour my hair for a big date and it went pink? I rushed round to her place and she plaited it up for me and arranged it under one of her hats so it was hidden, even though it messed up her plans for the evening."

For another half hour, we remembered some of the many nice things Emma had done for us, the times she had been on time, and the occasions she hadn't through no fault of hers. We all knew that usually it had been her fault, but that no longer seemed important.

At a minute to ten, the door opened again. We turned, without much hope, to look. Emma stepped inside. Poor girl looked drained. I rushed over and helped her to our table.

"Sorry, I'm late, but I do have a good excuse this time."

She told us that when the fire alarm had sounded, she went straight to her deaf neighbour to check she'd heard it. The old lady had panicked and Emma helped her gather together her handbag and medication and head for the stairs. Emma then heard a child crying because it wouldn't leave its cat. Emma helped the mother catch the terrified creature. Once everyone was outside, she'd tried to re-unite separated families and reassure frightened neighbours.

"The fire brigade and police were wonderful, but it was scary as we didn't know where the fire was or if people were trapped inside. An evacuation centre was set up in the church hall and we didn't know who was there."

"Are people still trapped?" I asked.

"No. Everyone is out now. I couldn't come straight here, because the fire brigade needed to account for everyone first and I couldn't call as I lent my phone to people who were worried about their families and there's no credit now and my purse is in my flat …"

"Is your flat OK?"

"Probably, but I wasn't allowed in to check. They said most of them where fine; it's only the ones on the first two floors of the north side that have smoke and water damage. It turns out the fire was in the underground car park. As you can imagine, burning cars make a lot of smoke. Fortunately my Mini wasn't in there and I was able to use it to help ferry people, too frail or shaken-up to walk, across to the church hall. The fire brigade thought we'd be able to go back tomorrow, but they have to check it's safe first. I came here as soon as I could, because I knew you'd all be waiting …"

We talked over each other as we offered Emma a place to stay and the loan of clothes and anything else she might need. We topped up her phone credit, checked her car could stay in the pub car park, and bought her a large drink.

"Drink that and tell us everything," Cara demanded.

We asked Emma every question we could think of and bought her more drinks until she was too tired to talk.

"Come home with me," Melanie said. "I've got a spare room."

"Thanks. Sorry about The Plan for tonight; I've ruined

that. I think I could do with a girlie night out; could we try again next week?"

"Of course we could," Cara said. "Any night you like would be fine with me."

"Anywhere you like; I can always book a taxi if I need to," Tasha said.

"We'll get there early and have a drink waiting for whenever you can get there," Melanie offered.

"We don't even have to plan it now, we could just do something spontaneous, if you like," I said.

"Friday, here, between seven-thirty and eight," Emma said. "I'll try not to be late."

That was last week. It's eight fifteen and, except for Emma, we're all in The Frog and Bucket. The door is opening. Maybe that's her now; but if not, we'll wait.

3. Decision Time

Annette flipped a coin; heads. She'd email her acceptance of the course first thing Monday morning and look forward to a few days in a nice hotel. A single toss of coin was no way to make a decision though. She'd try for the best of three. It was tails the second time. She didn't try again; random chance had already said both yes and no, Annette needed one single decisive answer. Her mum would provide one.

Seven, two… Annette stopped dialling. At forty-seven she shouldn't be worried about Mum's opinion. In fact she wasn't; hadn't been for a long time. Not since Mum said it was silly to waste money having her hair coloured in a salon and persuaded her to use an out of date dye she'd unearthed.

"It's a much brighter red than I want."

"No problem, just wash it out sooner than usual."

Annette hadn't been keen, but Mum sounded so sure. The result was Barbie pink. A frantic call to the help-line number printed on the pack provided the information that washing out the colorant halfway through the process was a big mistake and she'd need to visit a salon to have her hair returned to a normal shade. The hairdresser talked her into a cut as well and Annette had been quite pleased with the result.

Annette should have known better. Mum once sent her into the rain with a dress edged in paper doily 'lace' and had tried to talk Dad out of working for a company that made mobile phones saying they'd never catch on. It was nothing short of reckless to do whatever Mum thought sensible.

She hadn't listened to Mum's advice on her job choice and that had worked out fine once she'd changed departments. She hadn't asked for Mum's opinion when Brian had proposed. She knew he was the right man for her. Annette was less sure about her best friend Lynda's suggestion of lilac as the wedding theme. Although Annette loved the colour, when she saw the photos she had to admit it had suited raven-haired Lynda much more than ginger Mum and auburn Annette.

Thinking about it, there were other things Lynda had been mistaken about. That car parking space she'd told Annette to squeeze into had not been big enough. Luckily on that occasion it was only her pride and not anyone's paintwork that was damaged. If she asked Lynda's opinion about attending the course, Lynda would ask whether Annette could claim expenses and advise sampling half the cocktail list and not even ask which course it was.

Annette's kids were sometimes reliable, except when it suited them not to be. They'd realise her absence for a couple of days would mean their cleaner / cook / chauffeur / laundry-woman / bank / agony aunt would be unavailable and therefore tell her to stay at home.

Her beloved Brian was very sensible, but tended to say whatever he thought she wanted to hear. 'Either would be fine,' was his response when she couldn't decide which dress to wear and 'I like both,' when she couldn't decide what to make for tea. 'It's up to you, love', would be his reply about her current dilemma. What good was that?

She could ask one of her work colleagues. The people she worked with should know if it would be of benefit to her.

"Yes, go for it," was the advice of the first person she

asked. "If nothing else, it's a couple of days out the office."

When she tried for a second opinion she was told, "I should think you'd find it very helpful, but it's up to you."

That was a bit vague, maybe she should ask someone else.

Another colleague attracted her attention at the water cooler. "I hear you're still not sure about the course. I attended it myself and it's really good. You'd better accept while there are still some places left."

Annette, realising she'd been putting off making a decision until it was too late, sent an email to accept the place she'd been offered. Aaaargh! She shouldn't have sent it without thinking it through! Frantically she typed 'recall email' into the help box on her computer. She was too late; a ping announced an incoming email titled 'booking acknowledgement'. Reluctantly, she opened the message.

'Thank you for booking our assertiveness and decision making course. Your travel details are attached.'

4. A Lesson Learned

Maria hadn't been home much in the eight years since she left St Mark's School behind. Maybe it was her pregnancy making her nostalgic, maybe she was responding to a nagging doubt. Whatever it was, she'd had the urge to visit places from her childhood and gone to stay with her mum for a couple of days. When the baby's movements woke her that morning she'd decided, on a whim, to get the bus to school.

"They've changed the routes now," Mum warned.

Maria walked to the stop, looking for familiar landmarks. Towards the end of the street was the home of old Mr Harvey. His was the smartest in the street back then and the neighbours accused him of having airs and graces or thinking himself above them. Not Maria's mum; she said he was a good example. Maria had sided with the neighbours.

Why was she thinking about Mr Harvey now? He certainly wasn't someone she wanted to remember. He'd made life hell at school, and at home because it was impossible to escape him. He'd caught the same bus in as her every morning. He was there all day, of course. The journey home was Mr Harvey free as he stayed on after class, making big red marks on her essays and thinking up the most boring stuff to teach them. He'd been back in the evenings when she wanted to go out; a permanent reminder to Mum that Maria had homework to do.

'Manners maketh man,' had been Mr Harvey's almost

constant chant. Pupils had to raise a hand to speak and were made to address him as 'sir'. They were expected to stand aside if he walked toward them in the corridor, and rush to open doors for him. They had to say 'please' if they wished to use text books or even the dictionary. When he returned their homework they had to thank him, even when he'd given a really low mark. Daring to speak with food in their mouths when he presided over the dining hall resulted in a week of detention. Maria had seen it all as evidence of him being a child-hating snob.

Maria caught the bus outside the house where Suzy, her best friend from school, had lived. They'd exchanged Christmas cards since and attended each other's weddings, but otherwise lost touch. Suzy still lived in the same town. Maria might look her up.

As Maria looked for a seat she spotted a man who looked like Mr Harvey. She wondered if her memory was playing tricks. Then he spoke.

"You boy, get out your seat and let this lady sit down. Can't you see she's expecting a baby?"

There was no mistaking him then. Nor any mistaking the expression on the boy's face. Clearly he didn't think he should give up his seat, just because old Mr Harvey said so. She knew how he felt, because Mr Harvey had done the same to her in the past. Now she had a chance of revenge.

"No, it's OK, you keep your seat," she said to the boy who'd grudgingly risen. "You were here first and I'm fine standing."

Some children began to nudge each other and giggle. The boy looked concerned and gestured toward Mr Harvey.

"Oh, don't worry about what that rude man says. I think he's just trying to embarrass me by pointing out I'm a bit fat."

She thought she'd done well when she heard laughter and saw the boy smirk at Mr Harvey. The man himself looked sad, as well he might. He'd been the least popular teacher when she went to St Mark's and it seemed nothing had changed. Perhaps Mademoiselle Le Chevalier was still teaching. Maria couldn't now speak a word of French, but she had happy memories of those chaotic lessons.

Maria squashed herself against the side of the bus as they reached the school to allow the children to stream off. Mr Harvey followed them. He gestured for her to precede him.

"After you, Maria."

Belatedly it occurred to her he'd probably heard from her mum that she was pregnant. She guessed he'd wanted the boy to be polite to her so she'd see it from the other point of view. If she'd smiled and thanked the boy, Mr Harvey would have been pleased, the boy would have learnt politeness was appreciated, and she wouldn't have been left feeling guilty and with a sore back from standing as they drove over the speed-bumps.

Only then did she see how much she owed him. Her family hadn't been well off and she didn't find studying particularly easy, so her chances of further education had been slim. Having Mr Harvey's beady eye on her meant that, unlike some of her friends, she could never bunk off school. He'd been her tutor as well as English teacher, so it wasn't just in his lessons he'd had the power to make her pay attention. She'd got good grades. Those and her nice manners helped her get a job on reception in Westerfield Lodge, the nearest the town had to a swanky hotel. She'd been able to fit the hours around further studies and eventually qualified for, and obtained, a good job in hotel management.

She'd learnt a lot, but not the thing he'd tried so hard to teach her. Making Mr Harvey look a fool in front of his pupils most definitely hadn't been polite. Maria gave herself a mental shake. He'd ruined her teenage years, she wouldn't let him ruin today as well.

As she was already wallowing in nostalgia, she decided she'd revisit happy memories. It didn't take long to track down Suzy's number and give her a call. Suzy sounded really pleased and urged her to visit. Maria felt guilty again. Suzy fell pregnant at sixteen so couldn't continue school. She'd got married to the father of her second child just three months before the baby was born. The man worked as a mechanic's assistant and barely earned enough to pay the rent on their two bed-roomed flat. Maria had only attended the wedding because she'd already arranged to visit her mother that week.

Maria wondered what Mum's neighbours thought of her now. Were they impressed by her success or, because she rarely came back, did they consider her a bigger snob than they'd thought Mr Harvey? If so, they'd probably be right.

She caught another bus, into town this time and the mall which had drawn her and Suzy every weekend. It might seem patronising to buy Suzy expensive gifts, but it should be OK to get something for her kids. How old were they now?

In a toy shop the assistant answered her mobile and chatted about her date, including quite explicit details, before serving Maria. If she'd seen a member of her staff at the hotel behave in such a way, she'd have taken immediate disciplinary action. The woman was about Maria's age, but she didn't recognise her. Presumably she hadn't attended St

Mark's.

"Can I help?" the assistant asked without a word of apology regarding the call.

"I don't think so," Maria said.

Fortunately, the town's only other toy shop had friendly, helpful staff. A young man helped Maria select clothing and toys as well as a book for Suzy's oldest child. Maria thanked him warmly and left.

She stopped to rest in a cafe. As she sipped a reviving cup of tea, she saw small children snatching at food, with no words of thanks. She heard bad language used in front of them, so maybe it wasn't surprising they behaved badly with such poor examples to follow. Suddenly Maria wasn't looking forward to seeing Suzy.

Her friend was really pleased to see her and delighted with the gifts and Maria's pregnancy. She proudly showed Maria round her small, but immaculately kept, flat and introduced her to the children. They baby was just starting to talk. Suzy encouraged him to lisp 'thanks' when he was given his presents. The older boy said 'hello' and put down the game he was playing. It was clear he wanted to grab his gifts and rip off the paper, but he managed to thank her politely before he did so.

Maria said, "Your children are sweet and have lovely manners." She patted her belly, "I hope mine will be as charming."

"I'm sure he will. Set a good example, that's my advice. Start early. It might seem easier if you give in all the time and let them do what they want, but it's no help in the long run. Be really careful what you say too. They pick up rude words twenty times as quick as good ones."

Tears filled Maria's eyes and she hugged Suzy. "Thank you. I hadn't realised until now, but I've been worried I won't be a good enough mum."

"You will. I'm doing OK aren't I?"

Maria nodded.

"Well, you were always better at everything than me. You'll be fantastic."

"I'm not always good, Suzy." She told her about the encounter with old Mr Harvey that morning. "I'm going to go round now to apologise and thank him for his efforts in teaching me."

"That won't be any fun!"

"No, but it will be polite and I want him to know that I've finally learnt the importance of that."

5. Slightly Distracted

"Thanks love," Abbie murmured when her husband brought her tea in bed. She glanced at the clock. "Why didn't you wake me earlier?"

"It's your day off. I thought you'd like a lie in."

"But I have loads to do."

"You don't. Cousin David won't mind if you haven't washed the light bulbs, arranged the spice rack alphabetically, or whatever you actually end up doing today."

Abbie whacked Lance with her pillow. "Cheeky. That won't happen today. I'm going to be organised and not get distracted."

"OK, I believe you."

Clearly he didn't and who could blame him? But this time she really would do the things she had planned. If she concentrated on one thing at a time she'd be fine.

"Do you really think the light bulbs need cleaning?"

"No!"

"Not washing I don't mean, but they must get dusty, especially now we've got energy saving ones and they last so long."

Lance banged his head on his arm in a theatrical manner.

Abbie giggled. "OK, I'll leave the light bulbs alone."

"Good. Now try to enjoy your day off love, and please

don't worry about David. Honestly there's absolutely nothing you need do for him. I've forwarded you his email, which gives all the details." Lance kissed her and left.

Easy for him to say not to bother doing anything for David. He'd been so good to them and so much fun when they'd visited him in America. She planned to make him equally welcome in their home.

Abbie leapt out of bed. She couldn't find her electric toothbrush. Last night she'd noticed it needed charging but it wasn't plugged in. She remembered it had been windy and she'd gone out to fold the chairs on the balcony so they didn't get blown about. Sure enough the toothbrush was out there, tucked into a flower pot. Some of the lobelia and petunias were past their best and the compost was rather dry.

On her way back to the bathroom, with faded flower petals in hand, she remembered the mug of tea. It was cold so she made another and some toast. Fortunately the toaster was automatic and her bread didn't burn whilst she watered the pots on the balcony and then the ones in the windowsills. The butter didn't melt when she spread it on her cold toast though. She almost started the computer to read David's message as she ate her breakfast but stopped herself just in time. The computer could keep her distracted for hours!

The most important task was to get the spare room ready. She went there straight away, stopping only to put clean towels in the bathroom, and take the used ones down and put on a wash. As she stood up from doing that she noticed the book she'd been reading yesterday. She'd closed it without using the bookmark. She'd just find the right page, insert the bookmark and put it away. It wouldn't take a minute.

Two hours later Abbie had finished the book, but not even looked at the spare room. She'd just have a coffee and then start. By the kettle she found her toothbrush. Better plug it in or it would be good for nothing tonight. Unlike the items she'd intended to take to the charity shop; they'd be useful to someone. She'd put them all ready last weekend and then the phone had rung which distracted her.

Abbie, determined to do the job this time, took the bag straight out to the car. She'd have to drive past the recycling centre so it made sense to take the empty bottles with her. As she went in to collect them the post came. She'd just take a really quick look.

It was lunchtime when Abbie carried the recyclables to the car.

Her neighbour spotted Abbie. "I'm just going to make myself an omelette, fancy joining me?"

"Yes please." Not having to cook and wash up would save time. Over lunch she told her neighbour she was going into town.

"Can I cadge a lift?"

"Of course," Abbie agreed.

When the two of them got home the empty bottles where still in the boot of Abbie's car, her toothbrush was on the dashboard, rescued from the charity bag, and Lance was back from work.

"You're home early, is everything OK?"

"Yes, fine. Have you had a good day, love?" he asked.

"I have. I bought David some proper English muffins, crisps and biscuits. You remember how he teased us when we used the wrong names over there?"

"I do. It'll be fun to get our own back."

"It will and I'll look glamorous when we do. I've bought a wonderful bargain from the charity shop." She held up a carrier bag. "A designer dress and matching jacket in exactly the right colour for me. It was so cheap I didn't feel guilty about visiting other shops to find shoes to match. Don't worry, Sue from next door was with me and stopped me getting carried away with a bag and hair thingies too."

"Oh good. I was worried you'd spend all day getting ready for David."

"Well I haven't. Actually it's a good job you're early, you can help me."

"I'm not sure what I can do in the ten minutes I saved, but it doesn't matter as there's nothing to do."

"There is. His room's not ready and… ten minutes?"

"Yes. The roadworks are finished at long last."

"But …" Abbie looked at her watch, then at Lance's. "I can't believe it's so late." She raced along the hallway and back, still holding her toothbrush. "Can you get something out the freezer for dinner?"

Lance took the toothbrush from his wife. As she rushed away she heard his voice but didn't allow herself to stop and become distracted by his words. She snatched pillow cases from the airing cupboard before turning to crash into Lance.

"Abbie, calm down."

"But I've got to get ready. Heavens! I don't even know what time we've got to collect him from the airport."

"He'll be here in half an hour."

"What! Why didn't you say? I'm not ready!"

"I did say you didn't need to do anything and I forwarded his email."

"I didn't look in case I got distracted by the internet. You know what I'm like when …" She trailed off, distracted by the sight of her toothbrush in its charger. How had that got there?

"Abbie, listen. Cousin David says everything is on his company expenses so he's got a hire car to drive himself here, is booked into the local hotel and wants to meet us there for dinner, his treat. Now go and get changed into that outfit you bought today. Do not do anything else on the way!"

6. Wednesday Afternoon

I'd taken off my glasses to wipe away the rain, when my highly trained senses alerted me that something was wrong. I didn't have to see them to realise my enemies were planning an ambush. On a school bus, there's nowhere to run, no hope of hiding. I was greatly outnumbered and if I unleashed one of my devastating, super secret double-agent moves, I'd break cover and my earlier efforts would be for nothing. Was it worth the risk?

The gang lying in wait for me had made an earlier attempt to get hold of the formulas in my backpack, but the bell signalling the end of the lunch break had distracted them. I'd seized my chance to get away and, I hoped, lay a really clever trap of my own.

"Come on, Milky Bar Kid," Big Baz said to me. "Hand it over."

Tempting as it was to just do what they wanted, I worried they'd be suspicious if I did. I was still wondering what to do when I saw Natasha getting out of her seat. If she got involved things would only get worse for both of us. Before she could try to help, I handed over the exercise book I knew they wanted.

"Got any money?" Baz snarled.

I'd made it too easy and he wasn't satisfied. Although I did have some cash, I shook my head.

"Bet you have. Search him, lads."

They'd barely reached me when I discovered an ally. The bus driver hit the brakes and leaned out to face us.

"Oi, you lot! Stop messing about and get back in your seats if you want to get home tonight."

The rest of the journey was uneventful, except for Baz, and those of his mates who're in my class, copying out the formulas I'd spent nearly the whole lunch break writing. Then they ripped up my version.

When the bus reached my stop, Natasha was first off. I saw her putting up her hood as though she was getting ready to run through the rain, but I guessed she'd be waiting for me. I think she's nice, but I'm not sure. She seemed it when I first met her last September. That's when when we both started secondary school.

It was sunny that day, so easy to see we were in the same uniform.

"Hello," she said. "Are you in year seven too?"

I nodded, liking that she thought I could be older.

"I'm a bit nervous. Are you?"

I shook my head. I wasn't and anyway, boys don't admit things like that.

She talked to me every morning after that. Natasha likes Dr Who, James Bond and Terri Time Traveller just as much as I do. Sometimes we'd chat about what we'd do if we were one of the companions or part of Team Terri and make up adventures. We were the only two in our year who waited at that bus stop in the morning, so nobody knew about it.

Usually when someone seems like they want to be my friend it's some kind of trick. Most often it's so they can copy my homework or get me to do all the work on a project we're supposed to share. Sometimes it's to make me look stupid so they can laugh. Sometimes to get something from me. As you can tell from what Big Baz said, I look like the Milky Bar Kid and some boys kept on at me to say, "The Milky Bars are on me." I thought if I did they'd just laugh then leave me alone, but they said I owed them all chocolate. I had to pay over my lunch money all week.

There wasn't anyone I could tell. It wasn't like proper bullying so I didn't think teachers could do anything. Mum and Dad have enough to worry about. Dad didn't have a job for a long time and we had to move out of our house into a flat. They both work now and often don't get in until seven. I told them it's OK because I'd stay at friends. Didn't used to mind as I went to the library and read, but I've read most of the books now and anyway Natasha goes there on Wednesdays so I can't really.

You see she knew about Baz's gang being mean and tried to stick up for me. That just made them worse and if we were anywhere near each other they'd chant, "Natasha loves Jacob, Natasha loves Jacob." I've avoided her since then, but she still tries to talk to me. Why would she do that?

"Jacob, are you going to the library?"

I was right, she had been waiting for me, but that didn't help me know what to say.

"We could get a hot chocolate together if you are. I've got enough money for two."

I nearly said I had my own money, but that didn't seem like a good idea. If she was trying some kind of trick it would leave me wide open, and if she wasn't it might seem rude. If she really did want to be friends I didn't want to behave like some people had when I'd tried to make friends with them.

"Nah, you're all right. I'm going to my mate's house," I

said.

She looked a bit sad. "Oh, OK. Well, if he's not in or anything I'll be in the library until closing time."

I went to look for somewhere to get out the rain and saw a sign saying 'Art Exhibition. Free Entry' so went there. Just inside the door was a big see-through plastic box with money in. A man who was coming out put in a fiver. If they'd tried to make me pay I planned to point out the sign and tell them it was against trades descriptions. Might as well look round first though, I decided, especially if I was going to have all that hassle.

It was all modern art paintings, showing a variety of styles and influences. I know that because there was another sign saying so. It didn't seem any more honest than the 'Free Entry' one because each painting had its own little sign with the name and who painted it and a date. None of them were modern. Some were from even before Mum and Dad were born!

I couldn't tell what some of them were supposed to be. A few just looked like scribbles or as if they were painting something proper and then tried to cross it all out or paint over it. It wasn't fair,. If I did that people would say it was a scribble or I hadn't finished and it'd be thrown away or I'd have to do it again if it was in art class, but if someone famous does it then it's art and they keep it and put a frame on it.

I thought one was just all painted black. I read the little sign. 'Dark blue with black border No 37.' When I looked at the painting again I saw it really was dark blue in the middle. Really, really dark blue and you wouldn't even know it wasn't black except that the edge was even darker. That was sort of clever. I thought maybe if I read the titles of the others they'd make more sense.

One just looked like a bit of creased up paper. It was called 'Folded Paper'. That was true, but it didn't exactly help. There was something written in really faint pencil at the bottom. Hoping that was interesting I tried really hard to read the writing. It was just some stuff about the angles of the creases. I couldn't see what difference it made which way he folded it, it was still just a bit of creased up paper.

One was a plain background with wonky lines up and down. The little sign said it was an example of post modernism and called 'Repetition'. That made no sense at all. Post means like a goal post or letters the postman brings or, when it's with other things, it means after, like a post mortem to see why people died. Modern is now, so post is after now. When I thought that I guessed the artist was a time traveller. I checked the date it was painted but it wasn't in the future or even now. It was painted ages and ages ago. It should have been called pre modern really. It was all stripes but they weren't really repeated as they weren't the same. If he'd used a ruler it would have been better.

Right by it was one with lines which were properly straight. It was boring. Maybe it's true what Dad says about art imitating life because it seems you can't win with painting either. Make things different and it seems like you've done it wrong but be just like everyone else and you're really boring.

There was one with a woman who hadn't got any clothes on and her boobies were huge! Good thing she was sitting down or she might fall over, I thought. And why was she just sitting like that in the kitchen? She hadn't even got slippers on. It was so silly I couldn't help giggling.

An angry looking women tutted. "Some people shouldn't

be allowed in to ruin the experience for others," she said to another woman who was probably her daughter, even though she looked older than Mum and just as tired. Mrs Angry was doing that pretending to whisper thing but wanting to make sure people heard.

A man in a leather jacket grinned at me. I was surprised because he looked like the sort of person who'd pick on someone like me. I thought he could understand the picture was silly because he wasn't old, but his girlfriend didn't look like she could have left school long ago and she tutted too and dragged him away. Maybe women don't like boobies and that's why lots of them are always cross?

The angry woman seemed even angrier when someone else came in. I thought she was going to go up to him, but she changed her mind and turned away. He looked quite old and really scruffy, with horrid hair and a nasty beard and clothes which were even worse. I was pretty sure he'd smell and even more sure he was homeless.

The angry woman seemed to think so too. "Look at the state of him!" she said to her daughter.

"I think he must be sleeping rough, Mum."

"Exactly! It shouldn't be allowed. Something should be done. I shall write to the council and our MP."

They kept away from him and I did too. Mum said homeless people can be bad and I should keep away if I'm on my own. She sometimes buys them a sandwich though because sometimes it's not their fault they don't live anywhere and haven't got food. You can't always tell.

There was a photo I couldn't see properly because the angry woman had got in the way. I wasn't that bothered because it looked boring and anyway I thought a photo was cheating. I bet if I handed in a photo for my art homework my teacher would say it was. I decided to ask her – if I could do it when no one else could hear.

I moved on round a bit and found something which, although it was hung up like a painting, was more of a sculpture. That was OK, because that's art too. It looked like one of those maze things where you have to step on the right square to get out and if you don't then it gets you and you die gruesomely, or you fall through the floor but if you do you get the treasure and save people and are a hero.

Thinking of getting hold of treasure reminded me of the donations box by the doorway. There was a lot of money in it and no one there to make sure no one tried to nick it. I decided I'd better keep an eye on it. I wasn't the only person doing that. The girlfriend of the leather jacket man kept looking at it and I didn't think it was because she wanted to put anything in.

Because I didn't want her to know I was on to her, I carried on looking at the paintings. I'd got to some better ones by then. At least they looked like proper paintings. There was one of a girl with a violin. I think her gran must have knitted her jumper and it was probably itchy. The girl looked all right. As though she'd just carry on playing her violin and not take much notice of anyone else.

The woman in the next picture didn't look like that at all. I didn't like her. She reminded me of Aunty Jill. Dad calls her Winebox Jill, which Mum says isn't funny and he says no, she's right it isn't. I'm not supposed to know about that or that it's because she drinks lots of wine and forgets where she lives and has to go home with one of her boyfriends. She says I'm a loner like her and we both escape in different ways. I said that wasn't true and Dad said of course it wasn't and did I want some biscuits. When I went to get them he followed me and asked if I was all right and I'd made friends at the new school hadn't I? I said yes and when he said they were welcome to come round at the weekends I said I'd ask them and then I took my biscuits upstairs and stayed there until Aunty Jill had gone.

All those girls together in the next picture looked like they were friends. I could only see their backs because they were all watching a lot of boats. I think it might have been a race. There was space for someone else to stand and watch too, but I didn't think they'd want me too. If they saw me coming they'd all move up a bit and there wouldn't be room any more. Just like when I think there's a space on a table in the dining room at school. Why do they do that? It's not like I expect them to talk to me or anything. I just want to sit down and not be picked on and for that I have to find a table where no one knows me.

One day Natasha said to sit with her. I did but it was a mistake. Boys from my class came and sat with us and started doing, "Jacob loves Natasha, Natasha loves Jacob". She only went and told them to shut up so of course they did it for weeks afterwards. That's why I can't sit with her at lunchtime or on the bus or anything.

Next to the painting of the girls was one of lots of people in the park. I quite liked it. They seemed like they could have been real once and I looked for a while trying to see who was with who and what they were all doing and guessed what they'd do next. I do that with real people sometimes, if I think they won't notice me looking. I imagine the people who pick on me getting splashed by a car going through a puddle, or a seagull pooping on them or them eating something really nice and it dropping on a dirty floor. That makes me feel better because it could happen. If it did I probably wouldn't be there to see it, so really it's better to imagine it.

One of the people in the painting of the park looked like he was supposed to be a policeman. I don't think he'd be very good. If something happened I'd have to help him. I can't see any bad guys about so it should be OK. None in the picture anyway. There were quite a lot of people in the art gallery by then. One of them could try and pinch all the money from the box by the door. I made sure that if they did I'd be able to see them and make sure they didn't get away with it.

The angry woman had gone round faster than her daughter. The daughter was looking at the girls who were watching the boats. I reckoned she probably wanted to go and stand with them. I was just thinking if they were real and she tried they would probably let her, when her Mum came and found her.

"Have you finished here?"

That was a stupid question. The daughter hadn't been all the way round. It was obvious she was interested, because she read all the little signs and looked at the pictures close up. Then got as far away as she could and then came back and looked closely again.

Mrs Angry was standing in the way of a painting of a ship I wanted to see. I could have said, "Some people shouldn't be allowed in to ruin the experience for others." I didn't because I'm not horrible and rude like her.

"Linda, are you listening to me?" Angry woman said.

"Sorry, Mum. Did you want something?"

"I'm famished. Let's go and have tea and cakes, that's if you've quite finished?"

She looked like she'd eaten enough cakes already. Mum says not to say things like that about people as it's unkind, but I wasn't saying it only thinking it. I was also thinking that as well as being fat she was unkind talking about cakes in front of that homeless man. She could have offered to buy him some instead, couldn't she? At least she moved and I could see the painting again.

It was a really good one. A navy boat with men manning the guns ready for action. If I was there I'd like to be the lookout. I'm good at noticing things, so I could do that and help the captain. In the picture it was getting dark so I knew we'd have to act quickly. There was no cover so it was a dangerous mission, but I'd have risked going up and firing the gun if it would have saved the crew and country.

I knew I couldn't though. The captain would call me back.

"You're too valuable to lose, Jacob. You've got the best sight and best memory of anyone. No one else could recognise the enemy in time. I need you by my side to advise me."

I'd do as he ordered and no one would know until afterwards. That will be when I get my medal and a teacher sees it on the news. Then they'll announce it in assembly and everyone will have to clap and they'll all want to be my friend then. But I will be too busy with all my real friends in the navy. Except none of that's real and I can't do any of that and I don't have any friends. I'm rubbish.

I'd been kidding myself the whole time and not just with the stuff about the navy. Even if I did see someone steal money from the donations box I'd be too scared to do anything. I wouldn't even try to trip them up and if I tried to shout probably nothing would come out. I do notice things though, that bit is true even if I do need glasses. Maybe giving the police a description of whoever did it might be useful.

The leather jacket man had his hand down by his side near the wall. He turned something over a few times, then he opened his fingers and let it fall out as though he were dropping litter and didn't want anyone to know it was him. It was a twenty pound note. For a minute I wondered if thinking about the money made me imagine it. You can't blame me; it was an odd thing for him to do.

Then just as I saw it really was money and how much, the homeless man bent down and picked it up. I didn't blame him. Actually I felt bad as I had money, not twenty pounds, but enough for him to have bought some chips and a hot drink. I'd been annoyed with Mrs Angry for not thinking of buying him any tea and cakes, but I hadn't thought of helping him either.

"Excuse me mate, you dropped this," he said and tried to give the money back.

"No, I don't think so." The leather jacket man looked embarrassed. I'd been right that he hadn't wanted anyone to see him drop it.

His girlfriend reached out to take it, but he said. "No, Cheryl, it's not mine."

I knew it was, but didn't say anything. I twigged the bloke who dropped it did it on purpose. It was his way of trying to give the homeless guy some money without it seeming like that. That was a kinder thing to do than that woman who was going to write to her MP. It was probably kinder than Mum giving sandwiches in a way because the man who found it would just feel lucky and not that he should be grateful.

They were all looking at me then and I suppose some of them realised I might have seen what happened. Before I knew what I was doing, I said to the homeless guy, "That's right, I saw it there on the ground but you got it before me, so it's your money."

"If you're sure." He looked puzzled but sort of happy too. He went straight out, probably making sure he was gone before anyone said he couldn't have it.

The girlfriend looked furious. "For goodness sake, Tony! If you've got spare cash you could have bought me those shoes I liked."

"I told you, that would just be throwing it away. I'm not daft enough for that."

I decided I wanted to have a look at a picture on the other side of the room and went over there straight away. I'd gone back to the blue square with the black border and it reminded me things aren't always as they first seem. The picture wasn't and the bloke in the leather jacket wasn't. The angry woman was though. As soon as I saw her I thought she wasn't very nice and I thought that even more by then.

I looked around a bit longer. The girl playing the violin was still playing the violin and not bothering about anyone else. The heroes on the ship were still manning the gun and doing fine without me. The girls were still watching the boats, but as I looked and imagined trying to watch too, instead of thinking they'd spread out so there was no room, I thought maybe one might move across a bit so I could get in. They weren't real so there was no way to tell.

Then I thought about Natasha. She was real and seemed nice. Maybe she really did want to be my friend? I knew there was a way to find that out.

It was still raining when I got outside the gallery. I ran over to the library. Natasha was there like she said. She was reading a Terri Time Traveller book and on the table in front of her was a nearly empty cup which looked like it had hot chocolate in.

She looked up at me.

"That's a really good story," I said, pointing to the book. "Don't worry, I won't spoil it and tell you how it ends."

"It's OK, I already know as I read it before. I come in here and read a lot."

"Me too. Mum and Dad think I'm with a friend."

Then I remembered I'd lied about that to her as well. She didn't say that though. Instead she said something amazing.

"You are now."

The most amazing part wasn't really what she said, but that I knew it was true. "Yeah, I am," I said. "I'm going to get a hot chocolate. Do you want another one?"

"Yes please."

I bought the drinks and brought them over and sat next to her.

"Jacob, I'm sorry I didn't stick up for you on the bus. They stole your chemistry homework, didn't they?"

"No, they fell into my trap."

I could see she didn't believe me. I nearly didn't believe I'd done it myself.

"At lunchtime I was making up a story about me and Terri going back in time and finding the person who invented homework and getting them to invent something better instead. Baz and his gang saw me and asked what I was doing."

"So they teased you?" she said.

"No. They would have if I'd told the truth, but I said it was my chemistry homework. They left me alone then. At first I thought I'd been lucky, but then I guessed they might come back and copy it, so I wrote lots of stuff which would look like the answers if you're as stupid as them."

She grinned. "Brilliant! And then they stole it and they'll all hand in the same, totally wrong, answers. They're going to be in so much trouble."

"Yeah. It'll be good for a bit, but then they'll know what I did."

"Hmm, yes. We need a plan. What do you think Terri would do?"

We haven't worked it out yet, but I know we're going to come up with something. Something really, really good.

7. It Could Be You

"Ouch! sh sh shuttlecocks," yelps Molly, rubbing her shin. Drops of blood are forming in the graze that has ripped her tights. Her shin is already beginning to bruise. She kicks the 'A' sign that caused her injury.

'It could be you,' is the slogan over the giant pointing finger. She had been dreaming of a big win rather than watching her step.

"Well that's your opinion," she mutters.

Molly has her own opinions on the matter. She would love to win millions of pounds of course, but a banged shin is the most likely outcome of any dealings she will ever have with the national lottery. Molly has plenty of luck, none of it good. The father of her child left her a week before the birth. He denied paternity and Molly decided she was better off without constantly trying to obtain the grudging payments the court might decide to award. Money is a constant worry, there are few treats but Danny knows his mum will always be there to care for him. Danny would not benefit from a father who has made it very clear he doesn't want a child.

Last month she was told her job is to be cut. She's not been employed long enough to gain a redundancy payment. It's important that she obtain another job quickly, she has her son to support and rent to pay. The interview is in half an hour and it has just started to rain. She's hoping to become a receptionist in a local dental practice. She can hardly arrive dishevelled and bleeding, but doesn't have time to go home to change. Briefly, she considers buying a pair of trousers, but this expense would mean that she and Danny would have no food until her penultimate pay cheque arrived. This is no time for rash purchases. Why does money have to force all her decisions?

She continues walking towards the dentist's surgery, passing a Save the Children charity shop. Could that be the answer? Danny is a child and he will soon need saving if she doesn't get the job. She explains her problem to the kindly looking lady assistant. Molly hires a suit from the shop, by leaving her own skirt as a deposit and making a small donation. It's agreed that she will clean the clothes and return them in exchange for her own.

Molly introduces herself to the heavily pregnant woman behind the reception desk and is offered a seat. Flicking through a magazine, she waits for her name to be called.

The interview goes well. Perhaps because of the incident with the sign she's forgotten to be nervous. The borrowed suit is smart and creates a good impression, as well as giving her confidence. If she is accepted and starts soon she will try to buy it.

"There is just one more person for us to interview. If you would like to return in an hour we will give you our decision then."

Molly spends a nervous forty-five minutes window shopping, before returning to the surgery. The receptionist smiles at her as she walks in. Molly wonders if that's a good sign, or if the woman is trying to soften the blow.

"You can go straight in," she's told.

"It is my pleasure to offer you the position," Molly is informed before she can sit down. "I would like you to start working with Amanda as soon as possible, so that you are ready to take over as soon as she leaves to have her baby."

It's arranged that Molly will start almost immediately. She is honest about her financial situation, even explaining about the suit. She's given a £30 advance, enough for the suit and a blouse from the charity shop, and a new pair of tights. There's even a little left over. Molly decides to buy a treat to share with Danny, by way of celebration.

Danny loves cakes; the kind that must be sliced and eaten with a fork, because the generous frosting makes them impossible to catch hold of. His grandmother provides them for birthdays. The only cakes Molly buys are the ones which are reduced in price because they are no longer fresh and moist.

She is almost confused by the choice. Should it be gooey carrot cake, with a soft topping, coffee and walnut, or Dundee cake covered in glazed fruits and nuts? All were tempting, but she knew it would be Danny's favourite, a chocolate cake, she took home. The only real choice was between the milk chocolate sponge, filled with cream and decorated with white, milk and plain chocolate buttons or an extravagant dark chocolate gateau smothered in chocolate truffle icing and studded with whole cherries.

Even after purchasing the rich, sumptuous cake she has some money left. She walks back to the newsagents with the badly placed sign. Her luck appears to be changing and she wants a lottery ticket. As she queues, she dreams of all the presents she could buy for her son and herself if she were to win a large prize. Molly would be able to live in a nice house instead of the damp flat. She could drive a car instead of struggling with buses. She could take holidays. As she fantasises she gazes at the display racks and spots some stickers, the type Danny collects. She would not have enough money for them after purchasing the lottery ticket. Danny never pesters her for gifts. He is a good boy who understands it's not possible to have everything he would like.

After tea, she sits on the sofa eating a large portion of chocolate cake with her son and explains all that has happened during the day.

"The new job will be better and the people seem friendly. And I'll get a bit more money because they want me to start early. I'll be able to do a few more hours each week, and still finish in time to meet you from school."

"You're the best Mum in the whole world," he says over the noise of the lotto draw. Molly switches off the television and hugs him.

She remembers the stickers and gives them to Danny. She doesn't care who wins the lottery, she already has everything she needs.

8. Perfect Timing

Charlotte smiled brightly at Billy when he arrived and assured him it didn't matter at all that he was a bit late picking her up. It really didn't. Knowing what he was like she'd asked him to come half an hour earlier than she thought she'd need to leave.

She smiled a little less brightly when he announced he had to drop something off at a friend's house.

"Ted's not been well so I picked up his prescription for him."

She didn't smile at all when he stopped suddenly to help a girl whose shopping bag had split. Billy gathered up the scattered foodstuffs and gave her a new bag from the boot of his car.

Charlotte and Billy arrived at the station five minutes before her train was due to arrive. She had her ticket already so if he'd pulled up right outside and she'd leapt out of the car the moment it stopped and ran, she might just have caught it.

Billy wouldn't hear of it. "I can't do that. Just let me park and I'll come in with you to carry your cases and see you get away OK."

Billy was only trying to help, she knew, and anyway giving in would be quicker than arguing. He seemed genuinely surprised that she'd missed her train.

"I'm sorry, I suppose I should have driven straight here.

Something always seems to happen though."

Something always did happen to prevent Billy arriving anywhere on time. Almost always it was him stopping to help someone in need, so it was hard to be annoyed.

"I'll go and see when the next one goes," he offered.

She tried to stop him, but it was useless. Nothing could stop Billy trying to help.

He soon returned with a bright smile that mirrored the one she'd earlier greeted him with. "There's another just after six."

"Is there?" Her cousin, Fiona, had said Charlotte needed to catch the five past five to make her connection. Fiona though was a bit of a fusser, so had probably over estimated the time it would take to change trains.

"Yes, it goes right through to Reading. This means we've got time for coffee and cake."

Charlotte enjoyed the Victoria sponge and latte much more than listening to Billy say how much he was going to miss her. She was already beginning to wonder if moving in with Fiona was her best option.

"If you need anything, you make sure you give me a call. Promise."

"Yes, thank you, Billy. I'll be fine with my cousin. She'll look after me."

"I suppose so, but so could I."

There wasn't anything she could stay to that. She reached over and squeezed his hand. He'd been her husband's best friend since before Charlotte had met either of them. He'd been wonderful when Hubert had fallen ill and had looked after both of them. He'd continued to care for her since her husband's death six months earlier.

"I'd like to marry you, Charlotte if you'll have me."

"Billy! I... I ..."

"Sorry, I know now's not the time to ask but I didn't have the nerve before. Now you're moving away I've got nothing to lose, have I?"

"This is a bit of a shock. I hadn't realised you felt that way. I'm flattered ..."

"It's OK, I didn't expect you to agree. Will you think about it though?"

She assured him she would and that in any case, she'd stay in touch.

Charlotte had plenty of time to think during the train journey. Fiona had worked out the most scenic route and advised her to travel on a Sunday when the trains would be almost empty. Charlotte selected a quiet carriage which she had to herself most of the way, but the speed of the train and her thoughts made concentrating on the views impossible.

She'd known Billy liked her and would miss her once she was living with Fiona, but she'd had no idea he was motivated by anything other than kindness and friendship. She'd miss him. Charlotte sighed. Was she making a mistake moving to the other end of the country?

She shook her head. Everything was decided. The house was on the market, her belongings packed and Fiona expecting her. It would be difficult to back out now and Fiona would be disappointed, perhaps even upset. Her cousin had assured her she was looking forward to the company and having someone to look after. Sharing the household expenses made good sense, as had selling the marital home which, although it contained many happy memories, needed a great deal of maintenance. It would be nice to see Fiona again. Charlotte had enjoyed all the holidays she and Hubert had spent down in Devon. Each year they'd had a wonderful time, pampered by Fiona cooking lovely meals and fluttering around making sure they were perfectly comfortable. Could she cope with all that attention on a permanent basis?

Charlotte glanced out the window as they reached a station. She checked her watch. Odd, they seemed to have travelled much further than she'd expected. This must be a faster train. She stood and reached for her bags so she'd be ready when they reached her stop.

"Allow me," a young man said. He brought down her cases for her.

"Thank you." Charlotte smiled at him.

Really she was very lucky, people always wanted to help her. As an only child, she'd received constant protection and encouragement from her parents. She married Hubert straight from school and he'd cared for her their whole, happy married life. Her pain at losing him had been eased a little by the support of wonderful friends and family.

They passed through the station before her stop, so Charlotte put on her coat and stood ready by the door. They passed through the next station.

The young man who'd lifted her cases returned, presumably from the toilet.

"Oh dear, were you expecting to get off here?"

"Yes. I was hoping to change trains."

"This one goes right through to Reading now, but you should be able to get a connecting train there I'd have thought."

Hoping he was right, Charlotte called Fiona.

"You just caught me, I was about to leave to collect you," her cousin said.

"Don't come out yet. I'm afraid I missed my connection."

"Oh dear. A problem with the train?"

Charlotte explained and added, "I'm sorry, but I don't now know when I'll arrive. I don't want to mess you about."

"Don't worry dear, these things happen."

"I'll give you a call once I know what's happening."

"I'll come out now anyway and wait, otherwise you could end up waiting on the platform for quite a while whilst I drive down."

True, but that way Fiona would be the one waiting at the station, possibly for a long time.

"No, don't do that, please. I'd feel guilty."

Eventually Charlotte persuaded Fiona to stay at home until she called. Then she went in search of the buffet trolley; it might be a long time before she could get a proper meal.

The train reached its destination just before nine that evening. It didn't take long for Charlotte to establish that she'd already missed not only the last train to where she'd arranged to meet Fiona but also the last one back home. She was stuck in Reading.

Charlotte opened her phone. Who should she call? Fiona who'd carefully worked out the timetable Charlotte had failed to follow and who would have to drive for hours in the dark late at night to collect her? It would be gone midnight by the time she arrived, flustered about the alteration to her arrangements. They wouldn't get to her cottage before three. Charlotte couldn't face that. She'd been thinking about her decision to ask Billy to take her to the station that morning instead of getting a taxi. She'd known it was the last train and he was usually late – maybe she hadn't really wanted to leave and subconsciously sabotaged her chances?

She'd better call Billy then. If the fast train took three hours to arrive how long would it take Billy to drive down? Charlotte would have to wait on her own all that time and wouldn't get back to her packed up home until the early hours of the following morning. That alternative wasn't practical either and, perhaps worse, might raise Billy's hopes before she'd had a chance to fully consider his proposal.

Fiona and Billy, whilst doing their best to help her, had in fact left her in an impossible situation. Charlotte looked around the station for inspiration and spotted an advert for a local taxi firm. She rang the number and explained her problem.

"Don't worry, love. Plenty of B and Bs around here. We'll get you into one, no bother."

The driver was as good as his word, taking her to an establishment that he'd heard several of his customers praise as comfortable and reasonably priced. The friendly landlady showed Charlotte to a pleasant room and recommended the local pub as a good place to get a meal.

"They serve up until ten so you'll be OK. I can call to book you a place?"

She agreed and made a call of her own to let Fiona know she was staying overnight in Reading.

Soon Charlotte's bags had been carried to a pretty room, she'd had a quick wash in the spotless bathroom and she was sitting at a table in a cosy restaurant contemplating a tempting menu. Things really hadn't turned out badly at all. Fiona had panicked about her cousin being all alone in a strange place, but Charlotte reassured her she was absolutely fine and would see her the following day.

Charlotte ordered garlic mushrooms to start. There was no one to be troubled by the smell on her breath that night. For her main course she choose medium rare steak, something she wouldn't have wanted to eat in front of her squeamish cousin. If she had room she intended to order dessert. Usually she declined as neither her husband nor Billy ever ate puddings and so she hadn't like to make them sit and watch her or put them to the added expense.

"Would you like to see the wine list?" the waiter asked.

She ordered a glass of rosé. It might not be quite the thing to go with steak but she liked it and didn't have to take anyone else's tastes into account as she would if she'd been sharing the meal and a bottle. The food, including her crème brûlée, was delicious, but she knew the novelty of dining alone would soon wear off if she were to do it every day.

Charlotte puzzled over what she should do. She really was looking forward to spending some time with Fiona, but felt trapped at the thought of living with her permanently. She would also miss Billy a great deal. Her decision to move had been made too quickly and before she'd known all the facts.

The following morning, she checked the train times and called Fiona to say when she'd arrive. She also called the estate agents and told them that although she still wished to sell her house, she wouldn't want to move out for six months. Charlotte wasn't going to move in with Fiona; not yet. She wasn't going to marry Billy; not yet.

Charlotte had never looked after herself, but did that mean she couldn't do so? She would give it a try after a few weeks' holiday with her cousin. She might not cope and want her cousin to care for her. She might fall in love with Billy and want to marry him. Before any of that happened though, she would give herself the chance to watch rubbish on television without worrying it would annoy anyone, to eat garlic, drink the wrong wine and possibly get herself into scrapes.

Charlotte smiled brightly. It didn't matter at all that she'd been a little late for her train: she was right on time to start her new life.

9. Inside

Impatiently I circle the room, trying to invent things to do. I rearrange the already tidy books, alphabetically by title instead of by authors as they had been previously. The Library service comes every month; they bring a selection of books to my door and ask what I would like next time.

"Anything, anything at all," I tell them.

The staff are always kind. They will sit and talk for a few moments. Sometimes they suggest books they think I will enjoy, or which might offer hope. I always accept the suggestions. These people would help me if they could; they do help, but cannot provide a solution. My own thoughts and behaviour keep me here. Only by changing them can I find release. Instead, they provide books. I always read them regardless of style or subject. Reading passes the time, but not enough of it. I finished reading them two days ago. Oh how I long to be able to just stroll down to the library and exchange them. I must wait.

With the aid of a moist tissue, I gently polish the thick shiny leaves of my rubber plant. I support the tough leaf on my palm as I carefully wipe down from stem to tip. It will be days before it requires watering again. If only I was able to go into the garden and mow the grass. Wasn't it Oscar Wilde who wrote from Reading gaol of, 'The little patch of blue that prisoners call the sky'? A little patch of green grass on which I could go and stand; that is what I would call heaven. The feel of the sun, the rain, or the wind upon my face; before always taken for granted, now almost forgotten. The seasons of the year come and go having no part in my life now.

I could look out of the window of course, but that is something I avoid doing. What does it matter if it is dry and bright? Why would I care if the wind howls? Snow or ice mean nothing to me, nor sweltering heat. It's all out there just beyond the kitchen door, but may as well be in some undiscovered valley surrounded by impassable mountain ranges. To me that would make it no less accessible.

I comb my hair and check my clothing for stray threads or specks of dust. Keeping neat and tidy has become so important to me now. Oh, I realise there is no one here to appreciate my efforts but at least in my own mind I know I'm sticking to some set of standards. No longer can I go out and select fashionable, flattering garments. Make-up is possible. There seems little point whilst I remain in here, but I will not neglect any detail that helps to raise my spirits, however slightly. More important perhaps is the fact that these things also fill time. A little powder and mascara are applied each day. Lipstick and eyeshadow are avoided though as I feel bright colour is inappropriate. I also wear perfume; this place seems to have its own peculiar smell; closed and suffocating. Whether it is real or imagined I cannot say, however I do know it's inescapable, at best covered with something sweeter. Today's choice is based upon violets; a comforting type of scent.

Perhaps I could write another letter? Is there anyone I can send one to yet? There is nothing new for me to write about. I've not been anywhere or done anything. If I have anything to say then I immediately write out reports to send to as many acquaintances and family members as I feel could be even the slightest bit interested. Sometimes I wonder how many of them are actually read. Older people are probably the most grateful recipients of my correspondence. The oldest and frailest rarely go out and will therefore, like myself, be bored and share my joy at any outside communication. Sadly arthritis or rheumatism makes the sending of replies difficult for many elderly people. The tedium of their lives in common with my own generates little in the way of potential content. Those with busy, exciting lives lack the time for writing to others of their experiences. Leading a full and interesting life ensures little conception of the pleasure a letter sent to someone in my position would bring.

My brother will come tomorrow, that at least is something to really look forward to. Bless him he comes whenever he can. It's such a long way to travel. If I could move closer to him I would. Obviously an impossibility under current circumstances. My dear brother, the only member of my family who never criticises me for my present situation. He understands no better than the rest. How could he when I don't myself? He never asks me again and again why I have brought myself to this. Never does he remind me of my life before. How sensible I was once, how cheerful. What a normal person I used to be, before. Not once has he questioned that small thing which went wrong in my mind leading me to this confinement. Maybe he doesn't wish to know. Blood is thicker than water; one day perhaps he too will find he loses control. Maybe he too will go from being a member of society to one of those forever inside away from life, from normal people.

Oh I am so bored shut up here in my prison. Prison! If only it were that simple. If I were a thief I could give back that which I had stolen. If I had lied I could confess and repent. If innocent and wrongfully convicted I could appeal for release. If guilty at least I would understand the reason for my captivity. One day my sentence would end and I would walk free.

The bars that hold me are not at the windows, but behind the frustration in my eyes. The locked door is not on a cell, but between the neat little pearl earrings I wear. The key turned not in a heavy lock and thrown into the well but buried far, far deeper in my mind. My prison not Holloway or Alcatraz but Agoraphobia.

10. An Exciting Opportunity

Olwyn opened her magazine and read her horoscope. 'Make the most of any exciting opportunities that come your way'. Did people need to be told that, she wondered. It wasn't likely she'd be offered any opportunities, exciting or otherwise, but if she did she'd certainly make the most of them.

She flicked through the rest of the magazine and closed it with a sigh. She didn't know why she bothered reading; it never applied to her. Advice on spicing up her love life wasn't of much help to a seventy-three year old widow. Recipes for feeding a large family on a budget were equally inappropriate and as for the foreign travel articles... Oh well, she did enjoy the fiction and the rest helped pass the time and was invaluable for planning her TV viewing. She highlighted every quiz show that was on. Hopefully, pitting her wits against the contestants helped keep her brain active. Sometimes the magazines contained an interesting article she could discuss with her daughter too. Just as well, as Olwyn's own life didn't provide any topics of conversation other than the weather and the trouble she was having with her hip. It was hardly surprising Tessa didn't want to spend much time talking to her.

Olwyn gasped. What a horrible thing for her to think! She really was turning into a grumpy old woman. Tessa came around at least a couple of times a week to see she was OK and check if she needed anything, and she called her almost every day. When she saw her next, which would be later that day, Olwyn would make sure she was a bit less boring and a bit more appreciative.

"You OK, Mum?" Tessa asked as soon Olwyn had let her in and given her a kiss.

"Yes, I suppose so," she said before remembering her intention to be positive. "Sorry love, of course I'm fine. Just a bit bored that's all. It's lovely to see you though, really made my day."

"Why don't you come shopping with me? I know it's not exactly exciting, but it'd get you out the house."

"I'd be in the way and hold you up. I can't walk as fast as you."

"No you can't, but we could chat as we walked, couldn't we? I never seem to talk to you properly."

Wasn't that just what she'd been thinking this morning? That she'd like to talk to Tessa about more than her health and the weather and that she'd grasp any opportunities to relieve boredom that came her way.

"If you're sure."

The drive to the shops was very pretty, especially along the side of the canal. Olwyn hadn't realised it was so close to her new home.

"When the weather is warmer, I might come down here for a walk," she said.

"Good idea. The doctor said gentle exercise would be good for your hip."

Olwyn enjoyed walking round the store too. What a good selection of different things they had. This was an opportunity to try some exciting new foods and Olwyn cheerfully made the most of it.

After paying for the groceries, Olwyn said, "Why don't we stop in the cafe for a coffee and a cake? My treat."

"That'd be nice."

As Tessa pushed the loaded trolley towards the store's cafe, Olwyn took a look at the magazine display. Maybe they'd have some she couldn't get from the newsagents. One with some interesting stories in would make a nice change from celebrity gossip.

"Nice to see you out, your hip better today, is it?"

Olwyn looked up to see her neighbour, Polly.

"Oh, hello. Yes, thanks."

"Perhaps we'll see you over the club soon then?"

"Perhaps," Olwyn said. "This is my… " She trailed off when she realised Polly was already walking away.

Polly looked back and called, "Tonight's the night, you know."

"What was that about?" Tessa asked.

"Oh, she's a neighbour. Nice lady, popped in to welcome me when I moved into the bungalow and calls in every now and again. She's always in a rush like that. Lately she's been trying to get me to go to the social club. I explained I didn't want to go by myself, but she didn't really seem to listen and suggested the quiz so I wouldn't have to sit on my own. Says it's usually quite busy and there'd be a team I could join."

Tessa parked their trolley in the space provided outside the canteen and the two woman joined the queue for food.

"It sounds like a great idea, Mum," Tessa said.

"Does it?"

"Yes. It'd be something different and a good opportunity for you to get to know your other neighbours."

"Well, I'll see how I feel this evening." Olwyn then turned her attention to the tempting display of cakes. "I can't decide between the coffee and walnut or one of those lemon meringue things."

"They do look good, don't they. Let's get both and have half each," Tessa suggested.

Olwyn enjoyed the cakes, but the best bit was talking to Tessa. The change of scene meant Olwyn could point out the alterations in the town centre since she'd last been there and that led on to reminiscences of taking Tessa to the shops when she was a toddler.

"I remember the time when you were little and I found all sorts of things that you'd picked up and pushed inside your buggy. I tried to take them back, but didn't know where you'd got them all from and couldn't help thinking that for every one I returned, you might be picking up two more."

They both had a bit of a giggle and Olwyn felt better than she had for months. Tessa was such a good girl who wanted her mother to be happy; she'd be so pleased if Olwyn were to tell her she'd been to the quiz.

That evening, Olwyn put on her good wool skirt, some lipstick and a brave smile. She walked over to the social club, her steps getting shorter and slower the closer she came. Once right outside, she stopped. Tessa would understand if she said she hadn't wanted to go, or was too tired. Olwyn nearly turned and went home again but hesitated a moment too long.

"Olwyn, you've come! That's marvellous," Polly called from the car park.

Olwyn waited for her neighbour and walked in with her.

"Now let's find you a team to sit with," Polly said, loudly.

"There's a seat here," a young man called before Olwyn could protest that she wanted to sit with her neighbour.

The young man brought her a chair and introduced himself and the rest of his team. They were all men and to Olwyn they all seemed very young.

Olwyn didn't know the answers to many of the questions, and felt a bit out of touch when her team mates all seemed to know details of footballers and pop groups that she'd never heard of. Still, the couple she did answer were ones they didn't get and they seemed pleased to get her input.

"One for you, Olwyn," they said when the question was about Clarke Gable or a soap opera.

One question was 'what's the first sign of the zodiac?'

"Olwyn, can you help us?"

She tried to picture the horoscope page from her magazine that morning. Aries, she thought had headed the list. Were the different signs always listed in the same order?

"What's the one for January?" one lad asked.

"Capricorn," Olwyn said. "My daughter's birthday is the tenth of January and she's a Capricorn."

The man began to write.

"I'm not sure that's what they mean though. I think it could be Aries. Sorry, I'm not sure."

They decided to stick with Capricorn as that was already written in. The answer was Aries.

Eighteen was the highest score. Olwyn's team, along with four others, scored Eighteen. They didn't do so well on the tie breaker.

"Don't be silly," one said, when she apologised for her mistake. "You said you thought it was Aries and we overruled you."

"Anyway, we've never made it to the tie break before," another assured her.

"Yeah, you were great. Promise you'll sit with us next week?"

"Well yes, I will if I come," Olwyn said.

On Tessa's next visit, Olwyn was surprised to note her tea had grown cold whilst she'd chatted about her evening out. Olwyn giggled, "and you'll never guess what they called the team. 'Olwyn and the toyboys.' What do you think of that?"

Instead of sitting back and smiling politely, Tessa was leaning forward in her chair and grinning as she replied, "I like it! And will you be joining your toy boys next week?"

"I will, but first I need to do a bit of research. Will you take me into the library for some books? If I'd paid a bit more attention to the horoscopes, we'd have won."

11. A Rubbish Job

"Missed a bit, love," some would-be joker said as I emptied another plastic sack into my cart and placed a fresh liner in the bin.

He was referring to the pile of burger boxes, cardboard cups and other rubbish heaped around the bin. Some people, it seems, think chucking rubbish somewhere in the direction of a bin amounts to disposing of it properly. Honestly, would it kill them to take that one last step so they could get it in?

I smiled at the man anyway. At least he'd seen past my grimy clothes to the woman below. Since starting this job I've not always been treated as a human being.

Emptying street bins isn't a glamorous job admittedly, but it's performing a useful service. You'd think people would be grateful someone's trying to keep the area nice. Some were. I'd had a few encouraging comments and this morning, while it was still frosty, someone bought me a hot chocolate. Boy, was that welcome! Others though treated me as worse than the rubbish I collected.

"Buck up girl," I told myself. The unpleasant ones were in the minority, just as they had been at school. I glanced again over to the woman sipping a coffee; Andrea, the school bully. She was probably the reason my usually sunny mood had passed through a dark cloud. Oh she'd not hit me or stolen my lunch money, the school made sure such instances were extremely rare. They couldn't prevent kids being plain nasty though.

Leaving school and getting a job freed me from her tyranny. Since then, if I've seen her about I've usually managed to dodge out of her way. She'd passed me half an hour ago and I'd kept my head down. As I watched, she stood and walked toward me.

Andrea sauntered over to my cart, lifted the lid and dropped in her cup as though doing me a huge favour.

"Thanks," I muttered. I'd have said it to anyone else, so why not her? She was obviously expecting it and I'd long ago learned it was easiest just to do what she wanted.

"Melinda! It is you!" she said, all fake delight at seeing me. "Saw you earlier and wasn't quite sure."

"Yes, it's me."

"I can't keep up with you. Your mum hinted you got a good job, but then someone told me you were working in a slaughter house. Can you believe that?"

I could, because I had spent a week there, which was all I could stand. That was none of her business though, so I asked, "Do you work locally?"

Andrea blinked for a moment. Maybe she was remembering it had always been her who'd asked the questions. She'd ask me what I thought of a boy I liked, right in front of him. Or what I'd be wearing to a party she knew I'd not been invited to.

"Yes, that's right," she said.

"You were going into fashion, I remember. Your coat is nice… Oh! You didn't design it did you?"

"Er, no. Not this one."

Of course I knew that. She's an assistant manager in one of the High street stores, one I avoid obviously. For a moment I felt mean for asking. I was all ready to say that reaching a management position at twenty-nine was impressive and that in these tough times it was something to have a job at all, let alone one in the area you'd always hoped to work, but she cut me off.

She was working for an international fashion house, she told me. I think she meant they had a couple of branches in Scotland, but didn't say. Apparently she was being fast tracked as well as constantly being begged to wear the company's clothes as she looked so good in them. That, I presumed, was her way of saying she had to wear the uniform, just like the junior staff.

"That's great," I assured her, putting real warmth into my voice. Saying nice things whilst thinking the bitchiest thoughts is a trick I've learned. I guess my guilt at being so uncharitable makes me compensate.

"And you? Always beavering away in the library, I recall and staying late to work on projects."

That was true. Mostly it was to avoid her. My social life's loss was my education's gain and I left school with good exam results.

"We thought you'd end up on Mastermind or something, answering lots of questions."

She hadn't thought that at all, but had teased me to that effect.

"Things didn't turn out that way. Almost the opposite, really."

Andrea glanced at my trolley and the litter grabber in my hand. "So I see."

"I will be on TV though."

"Really? I'd like to see that." She couldn't have made it more obvious she didn't believe me if she'd tried. Maybe she had been trying.

"Yes. There's going to be a series of reports on the BBC about people doing under appreciated jobs."

"Oh."

"I'm being filmed today as it happens."

"Oh?" One over-plucked eyebrow was raised.

I pointed out the cameraman. "Hey, would you like to be interviewed, Andrea? Might be interesting to contrast us. From what you've said you're obviously really appreciated."

The inner struggle was visible on her face. Poor woman clearly still cared far too much about what other people thought. She'd want to be on TV, but not associated with me. She'd enjoy the chance to brag, but knew she might be caught out.

"Nice of you, but I just couldn't steal your moment."

"No, I suppose not." I gave my sweetest smile. "I'd better get on. Do catch the show if you can."

"Yes, I'll do that."

Weeks later, as I sat down to watch, I was sure she would be too.

"Coming up next," the continuity announcer said, "Melinda Banks is doing a series of undercover reports on people doing unpleasant and unappreciated jobs. Watch as this up and coming journalist packs frozen chickens, inspects sewage pipes and learns what it's really like to be a traffic warden."

12. Time For A Change

'Miracle baby,' read the headline in the paper describing her birth. The reporter understood that the time, money and emotion Angelina's parents spent to create her had been worthwhile.

Everyone was interested. "She's so beautiful," they gushed over her crib. Total strangers sent money and gifts.

"Our angel, our precious gift," became her lullaby.

Encouraged by constant attention she thrived. Admiring adults clapped when she waved or grabbed at a toy. Angelina took her first steps weeks before some other children learned to walk. Her first clear words were uttered when many children her age were still unable to speak properly.

"Look how well she paints," Papa said as she smeared coloured goo on paper.

"She can write already," Mama cried when she scribbled with crayons.

Every skill she mastered was hailed a triumph, rewarded and applauded.

Then came school.

Angelina was not the only pretty girl. She was not the only child who could button her own coat. Some of the other pupils were reading before Angelina made sense of the letters. Most boys ran faster than she could. Overlooked, she rebelled, was expelled.

Her home tutor gave complete attention to his only pupil.

She had the neatest writing, the quickest answers, the best results in her class of one. Angelina learned fast.

Maintaining her novelty value was essential for maintaining what she'd come to crave; other people's interest in her life. She took jobs, never staying long. Being the fun, new girl gained her attention. Being just one of the staff did not. Papa bought her a shop of her own, but that was no good. Lots of businesses were run by young woman. Angelina wasn't anything special.

Her family lived in a big town. Many of the people she passed on the street didn't seem to notice her. They didn't know who she was, appreciate how special. Angelina persuaded Mama and Papa to move to a small town in the country.

They bought a big old house, painted it pink. People noticed. After the petition and visits from the council, the house was whitewashed. Interest in the new arrivals wasn't quashed.

The pretty new girl in town, with money to spend and friends to make, Angelina was always noticed and sometimes admired. Everyone knew who she was, she made sure. The admiration waned a little over time and the friends never became close, but she didn't care. She could make them notice her. She set tongues wagging with the shortness of her skirt in church, or the length of time she held the handsome young minister's hand after the service.

Angelina still wanted everyone's attention, but now there was one whose interest was of more importance to her than that of all the rest. She was an angel, it was only right a man of God should love her. The fact he was well respected, the secret choice of mothers for their daughters and daughters for themselves, was no bad thing.

As fiancée to the locality's most eligible bachelor, she was envied. The attention pleased her, but was not enough. As the future wife of the minister she should be respected and admired. Angelina changed. She visited the sick, assisted those in need, comforted the lonely. Her actions were not ignored. She won affection and attention in equal measure.

As the minister's bride she was fêted. The bishop himself conducted the service. Her bridesmaids were pretty, Angelina was radiant. The flowers and ribbons were light and bright, Angelina glowed. The champagne was bubbly, Angelina sparkled. There were pictures in the paper, a piece on the radio. Everyone was interested.

Now just his wife, she's almost ignored. Not by him. She's still precious to her husband, but he's just one man. To everyone else she's just another nice church wife, in a pretty apron, pouring tea, slicing cake. Nothing special.

Angelina attends the services. The usual Sunday ones are boring. The big ones; christenings and Christmas, weddings and funerals, Easter's rebirth, they interest her.

Pregnancy would create attentiveness, but not for long. Motherhood would provide a rival. It's she alone who must be the centre of interest.

Angelina makes arrangements to become a tragically young, beautiful widow.

13. Waiting On Freddie

"I know you," Freddie said as I handed him his menu.

Bang went my hope of hovering unnoticed in the background, as I'd planned from the moment I'd learned Freddie 'Fingers' Winson was a regular customer. I didn't think he'd clapped eyes on me since school, nor that he'd take any notice of a waiter. For a minute I considered brazening it out, but I gave what I hoped was a polite nod of agreement. I'm not much good at lying and never could stand up to him.

"Got any money?" he'd ask.

Other kids sometimes said no, but I never dared. Every week I'd meekly hand over the few coins Mum had scraped together for sweets or the bus fare on cold days. I had to walk whatever the weather in case Freddie wanted money when I had none. He'd make me pay one way or another. It wasn't just me; Fingers had dozens of victims.

"Never forget a face," he said. He ordered an expensive bottle of wine, then cracked his knuckles in the way I used to dread. That's not how he got his nickname in case you were wondering. That came from what he did with a stapler to my mate Jim when he wouldn't hand over a five pound note.

"We'll get our own back, just you wait," I promised him.

He did in a way. Jim, unlike Freddie, worked hard at school. He got a good job and has a nice house full of nice stuff. He bumped into Freddie a while back, in the restaurant actually, and told him all about it.

"It felt good seeing the greed on his face and to know he couldn't get his hands on it," Jim said.

"You want to be careful what you say to the likes of him," I said. "You don't know what he might do."

"Don't worry, I've got a pretty good idea. I have an idea about you too, Wayne. Reckon you can carry plates and pour wine?"

"Sounds easy enough," I said.

Jim got me this job. Let me tell you I was wrong about it being easy. Waiters don't just wait for people to decide what to eat, carry it out and wait for a tip. Oh no, we're rushing about here, there and everywhere, answering questions, clearing tables, juggling scalding hot plates and smiling politely no matter how rude the customers are. It takes a lot of effort to respond pleasantly when some drunk snaps his fingers and shouts "Oi"

Freddie was that type. I guess he would have been anyway, but he took extra trouble to be obnoxious once he recognised me.

"Plain Wayne! Knew I knew you."

His companions laughed at his witty way of referring to me and marvelled at his cleverness in remembering.

I marvelled a little myself. Not at his cleverness, a good memory isn't necessarily a sign of intelligence, but it surprised me I'd made enough of an impact to be recalled.

"You always reckoned you were better than me, didn't you?" Freddie demanded.

It's true, but I didn't say.

"Going to get some important job and get your own back, weren't you?" Freddie taunted.

I wondered if Jim had told him that. Jim's a good mate and a clever bloke, but sometimes takes silly risks. Sometimes they pay off, which is why he's done better for himself than I have. And sometimes they land him with his fingers stapled to his pocket money.

"So, you own this place do you?" Freddie asked.

"No," I admitted.

"Speak up, Wayne."

"No, Mr Winson, I don't own this place."

"Manager then?"

I swallowed my pride. "No. I'm just here waiting tables."

Freddie and his cronies found that hilarious.

"It's just temporary."

That was funnier still.

Freddie picked up a glass and casually dropped it onto the hard floor. "Ooops," he said. Then, "You watch your fingers," as I swept up the debris.

"Thanks, Fre… I mean Mr Winson, I'll be careful."

"You see you do."

They came in once a week and had me running to the kitchen querying ingredients, changed their minds constantly, demanded extra sauces and generally made a nuisance of themselves. One good thing was that Freddie liked to brag about how well he was doing and seemed keen to prove it by tipping generously. I wasn't too proud to take the money. He owed it me anyway, didn't he?

"See much of your old friend Jimmy, do you?" Freddie asked one night.

"Sometimes, Mr Winson." I didn't bother reminding him Jim hated being called Jimmy; I'm sure Freddie knew.

"Doing well for himself, I hear. Big house down by the river, thirsty car in the detached garage, pretty wife with cash of her own."

"I believe so, sir." Just how much did he know about Jim?

Freddie took a sip of the wine which cost him as much for a single bottle as I spent on a week's groceries. "I heard he's off to the Bahamas soon?"

"He did mention it, sir." I agreed with Freddie out of habit and only later thought that maybe I shouldn't have.

"Ever been to the Bahamas, Wayne?"

"No, sir. I haven't."

"Lovely place, though I don't think I'll be joining Jimmy there. What do you say, boys?"

The 'boys' all laughed some more.

The next morning I rang Jim and told him what Freddie had said about him going away.

"Don't worry, mate. I know he wouldn't have got the information from you," Jim said.

I was only partly relieved he'd taken it so well. "Be careful, won't you?" I warned.

Freddie really thought he was someone, but he was just a crook. Not just a wideboy I don't mean, but a real criminal. His weekly visits to the restaurant weren't social occasions with his friends, but planning meetings with his accomplices. Freddie thought I was a no one, so other than the occasional hilarious jokes at my expense and unnecessarily adding to my workload they didn't take much notice of me. I was, after all, able to carry out my plan of hovering pretty much unnoticed in the background, though of course always ready to spring forward when a click of the fingers indicated Freddie wanted something.

"Yes, Mr Winson? What can I get for you sir?"

Naturally I considered spitting on his food, getting chef to add laxatives or use out of date prawns, but I didn't dare. So I just carried on listening to his bragging and letting him treat me like I was less than the crumbs which dropped from his ever open mouth and accepted his tips.

That was until last night.

Last night I sat in the dark, in Jim's house. Sat just waiting. That might seem a surprising thing to do. Certainly Freddie and his gang thought so when they broke in.

"Plain Wayne! What the hell …?"

"That's Sergeant Wayne Cooper to you, Freddie. And this here is Inspector Jim Blaine, but you don't have to call us that. In fact you don't have to call us anything at all, as you have the right to remain silent …"

14. Where There's A Will

My solicitor asked to see me before the reading of the wills. "I doubt the outcomes will be favourable," he warned me.

For a clever man he's rather slow sometimes. I realised, even before he'd drawn up the first, that relatives of the dearly departed guests of Manor View Rest Home, managed by yours truly, would be furious when the wills were read.

"They are valid, aren't they?" They'd better be for what I'd paid him.

"Yes. I don't see how a challenge could possibly be mounted."

That was all I really needed to hear, but I said I'd go and see him anyway as that's what he wanted. I'm like that, always doing the right thing.

Take my sister Tracie for example. She's always whining at me over something, but do I complain? No, I run the business we inherited from our parents and give her half the profits. Half, even though I do all the work. All I deduct is my wages and expenses. Tracie doesn't see what's involved. She doesn't understand how I'm torn between providing a good service to my residents and making enough for us both to live on.

"You're a cheapskate," she told me.

"Really? Just take a look at this heating bill. Old people feel the cold. I keep all the rooms nice and cosy." It's horrendously expensive, but at least it keeps them quiet.

"You never redecorate though, or provide new furniture."

"The residents don't want the upheaval and inconvenience of that. They like familiarity and having their own things around them." That's perfectly true. Besides most of them have such bad eyesight they wouldn't notice new wallpaper or carpets anyway.

"You hardly have any staff so they don't have time to talk to the residents…"

"Lots of different faces would be confusing, besides chatting isn't what I pay my staff for. They're here to ensure the residents are clean and well fed, which they are. To ensure they get any medical care they require, that sort of thing. Conversation and social activities are the responsibility of the families …"

"And that's another thing," she butted in. Always interrupting me she is.

"Tell you what, Sis, if you're so worried you do a piece on this place for that newspaper you write for. Neglect of the elderly is a hot topic at the moment, isn't it?"

"You admit they're neglected then?"

"Yes, though not by me. The families dump people here, then all but vanish until the wills are read. It makes me so angry. They have a quiet little funeral, check they're the beneficiaries, then remove any possessions of value leaving me to dispose of the unwanted junk. What I charge for that hardly covers my time and expenses. Of course the care I've provided is unappreciated. That's why I make sure I receive payment in advance. Otherwise some bills would never be settled. At least relatives don't usually display sufficient bad taste to reclaim any unused advance."

I stopped then, realising I'd gone off on a tangent. I was

happy for my sister to write an article, all publicity is good and the free kind best of all. I didn't intend to be the focus of it though. Wills weren't something that need feature too heavily either.

"You're saying the ladies are abandoned by their families?"

"Some of them don't get visits even on their birthdays or at Christmas." I didn't mention the remote location, tiny car park or that visitors have to call in advance to gain admittance, as Tracie knew, these were simply security procedures. They didn't stop us visiting our parents when they lived at Manor View.

"That's awful."

"I know, Sis. I do what I can by spending time with them myself. They see me as a friend and would be sad and lonely without me."

She looked thoughtful for a moment. "OK, I'll do it. Maybe it will shame some relatives into taking a more considerate view of elderly relatives in this, and any other, home."

"Excellent." It would show I was on the level too. You see a lot of my residents had made new wills recently. It's true I'd spent a lot of my time talking to them and I suppose many picked up on, and agreed with, my poor opinion of relatives who didn't bother to visit. Those new wills state that if the bereaved hasn't received a visit from anyone other than staff in the preceding three months their estate will come to me. If there have been visits then everything will be divided among the visitors for that period and I'll get nothing.

It didn't take Tracie long to get the go ahead from the paper and come down and ask the residents if they were willing to be interviewed. Each of them was eager to talk to her. I suppose having someone prepared to listen and actually be interested in what they said was a novelty.

"Many of the ladies have led interesting lives," she said. "There's potential for a whole series."

War heroines mingle with activists for women's rights apparently. Who knew? Even the least among them have lived through, and contributed to, an exciting period Tracie pointed out. She got quite involved with the ladies for a time as she researched their lives. For weeks on end she drove down to Manor View and sat, notepad in hand, chatting to my residents. Hardly gave me a word, but then I was far too busy to talk to her.

For all her interest and indignation, Tracie didn't return to the home, or visit any of the ladies after she'd got all she wanted from them. A few said they'd seen her, but you know what old people are like.

When Tracie's article appeared, the residents all asked for a copy of the paper. Several copies most of them. I suppose they hoped to share it with visitors should they come. Naturally I obliged by collecting the papers for them. I didn't even charge more than the cover price despite it being a fair drive to the nearest newsagent's.

When I read my copy I saw she'd done quite a good job. The boring, restricted existence of the interviewees was contrasted with their earlier lives. She explained how they'd once struggled to achieve freedom for the generations to come and how those younger people now seemed to want freedom from them. It was heartbreaking stuff.

Very little was said about Manor View itself. Difficult to do that I suppose as she's a 49% shareholder. There wasn't much about me either, just direct quotes from my residents.

Very kind they were. There was a photo of each of them with a few biographical details and the promise of more to follow in a series of articles over the following weeks.

Everyone was in a buoyant mood, myself included. I asked the staff to bring all the ladies a glass of sherry that evening. We keep some to celebrate birthdays and other special occasions.

I overheard the cook say, "Reckon we should leave a few bottles. Least old skinflint can give 'em after all that free publicity." Not wanting to spoil an otherwise pleasant day with a reprimand about respect and economy I ignored her. That was a mistake.

My sister's words were in my mind. Spending evening after evening in a rest home might be my fate one day, but it didn't have to be my present. Hadn't Tracie said the staff who cared for my residents did all they could, despite difficult circumstances, to keep the ladies comfortable? They didn't need me checking up on them every hour of the day and night. That's what I told myself when I rang for a taxi to take me into town. I deserved a decent evening meal for a change. I go out for a good Sunday lunch each week, but otherwise take all my meals at Manor View. Not that I serve poor food, but I do have to keep costs under control. If I want anything fancy, I go out for it, and pay for it too.

I left my mobile behind. I deserved a few hours off from the pressure of being constantly on duty. If anything happened, the night manager would earn her money for once, instead of dozing in an arm chair through her whole shift.

There were still seats left for the next performance, a sign outside the theatre informed me. That seemed an omen, so I watched the play before dinner. The delay sharpened my appetite and I ate and drank with relish.

My taxi couldn't pull up in the parking space outside Manor View. That was blocked by a fire engine. Another had driven through the hedge and onto the front lawn. Police cars and ambulances lined the road.

There weren't any survivors.

It wasn't until a couple of days later that investigations, including autopsies, hinted at what happened.

"There will have to be a proper inquest of course," I was told. "But it seems there was a large quantity of paper near a heater in the communal lounge area. That's the likely cause. The victims all had alcohol in their systems which meant they would have slept more deeply than usual and any who woke would have had a longer reaction time. Mercifully it seems unlikely anyone did wake up."

I explained about the newspapers and the sherry. Wrong as it seemed to place any blame on the cook, who had clearly meant her action to be a kindness, the truth had to be told. She, and the cleaner I'd heard her speaking to, had left for the day and so escaped the blaze.

My solicitor assured me of what I'd known myself; I was entirely blameless. The heaters and fire alarm system complied with the necessary safety regulations. I knew because I'd had everything carefully checked before Tracie came snooping round. Thankfully my insurance policy was all in order and provided an immediate cash sum to tide me over so, although homeless and without a job, I wouldn't starve before the legal formalities were completed. Tracie would get half of that payout of course.

Once probate was passed and I inherited the estates of my deceased residents I would have plenty of money, none of which I'd have to share with my dear sister. The solicitor was due a cut for acting as executor. When we discussed the wills' wording I'd suggested he allow for a little more than his standard fee. He'd readily accepted and immediately forgotten any tiny doubts about the scheme.

The poor chap looked quite gloomy when I arrived. Almost as though he had bad news for me.

"You said those wills couldn't be broken," I accused.

"I believe that to be the case."

"What is it then? The inquest?" I didn't see how we could have anything to worry about there.

"No, no …it's the post." He indicated what looked like a pile of birthday cards. "As you know, all post for everyone at Manor View has been redirected to me since the fire, so I can deal with anything requiring attention."

"Of course I know." It had been my idea. I'd instructed the bank to stop requesting payments. That was the closest I wanted to come to communication with the relatives of my late residents.

"They all received one of these." He handed me a card from the pile.

It was from Tracie and contained a handwritten note saying how much she'd enjoyed chatting to the lady concerned the previous month and was looking forward to seeing them again, as usual, the next Sunday.

"I telephoned your surviving staff," the solicitor told me. "They confirmed your sister has been a regular visitor over the last few months. For most of your residents she was the only visitor during the final three months of their lives and therefore …"

He didn't have to say it; my sister was the beneficiary of all my carefully made plans.

15. Is It Time Yet?

Come and cuddle me again. Please oh please. You squeezed me yesterday, when nobody was looking. You held me gently when you felt how soft I am. You guessed, didn't you? Realised that bear you'd gazed at in the shop window when Granny took you to town was no longer sat behind the glass.

Is it time to open the presents yet? Surely it must be soon? The decorations have been up for ages and ages. I heard your grown-ups debating where each garland should go. The gifts wait under the tree, with the lights making my shiny wrapping keep changing colour.

Open me now, please. Oh go on, per-er-lease. Just me, the rest can wait a bit. You could just have a look, see what I am. There's no need to take me right out the wrapping, you could just look in. Well you could take me out. You could play with me. You know I'll be fun.

I've been ever so good, really I have and I asked Santa for a nice boy like you to be my owner. I'll be the bestest teddy a boy could have. We'll go exploring together, you can be a famous mountaineer and take me climbing really high. When you're a great detective I'll help you hunt for clues. When you're a secret agent, I'll be your lookout. When you score the winning goal, I'll present the cup.

We'd better try to sleep now. Tomorrow's Christmas, then our fun will start.

16. Breakdown

I'm just driving to work when my car starts coughing and spluttering the way it does sometimes. Like me, before my first coffee of the day, I suppose. The heat can't be helping, but it's an old car, a rather cute classic actually, so it's not surprising some things don't work as well as they could. You know what it's like when the car plays up; you think you'll get it sorted, but something comes up, or you don't have the cash or you worry the garage might try to cheat you. You put it out of your mind. You'll do it next week, or get your dad to take a look next time you see him.

I was a student until a few weeks ago; I've got a great job now, good prospects and all that. When I get paid I'm going to treat the car to a proper service. No pay cheque until next week though, so there's more muck than petrol in the tank. It's working its way into the carburettors I expect. It's amazing how much I've learnt in the last few weeks.

"Research common car problems, Janina," I was told by the boss. Today, if I ever get to work, my newly acquired knowledge will be put to the test.

I wish my mechanical knowledge was more practical. Judging by the noise my car is making, today is the day the grinding sound stops being a warning and becomes, 'I told you so'. There's nothing for it, I'm going to have to stop. I pull over and call work to tell them what's happened. They take it quite well.

"We've heard of people working from home, but not from

a lay-by in their car."

"You can't mean you want me to work here?" I ask.

"Yes, Janina, that's exactly what we do want. You've got your equipment with you, haven't you?"

I have of course, so at least there's no need to let my boss down. Staying in the lay-by isn't really an option, obviously I need a garage. Just as I begin to search for a number, there's a tap on my window.

A middle aged man in a shiny brown suit is standing by my driver's door. I wind down the window a little way, letting in a blast of exhaust and aftershave fumes, but no breeze.

"Got a problem, love?"

I nod and begin to explain. I don't get far before he interrupts.

"Good thing I'm here then. Wouldn't want a pretty little thing like you stuck all on her own."

Typical male chauvinist pig I think, but this isn't the time to tell him that.

"Soon get you sorted, sweetheart, don't you worry," he says.

I'm sure he'd have patted me on the head if the window had been open far enough. He seems fairly harmless, but you can never tell. I hope my perspiration is just giving me limp hair, not making my dress cling to my curves.

I phone work to let them know what's happening. I describe the man who has offered to help and mention the make of car he'll use to tow mine.

"Where's he taking you?"

My rescuer gives the address. He was perfectly happy for

me to call and there's nothing evasive about his reply, so I'm confident he really will take me where he says.

"Keep your wits about you Janina," my boss cautions.

"Don't worry. I'll call you later."

My red and shiny faced knight in drip-dry polyester opens his boot and brings out one of those solid towing bars. After fixing it in place he says, "There's no need to be scared, all you need to do is steer. Don't try putting it in gear, darlin' and don't forget to take off the handbrake."

Yeah and don't forget to be grateful whilst you're being patronised. I suppose that's not fair, the guy is trying to help. Getting towed in by the garage would probably set me back £150.

At the garage, I retrieve my heavy work bag from the back seat and hand over my keys. I'm given a plastic cup of disgusting tea and told to make myself comfortable. The orange plastic chairs aren't very relaxing, but I have space to put my laptop and begin typing up a report. There's air conditioning too, so I'm prepared to forgive quite a lot, even the 'hot babes' calendar on the wall. A glance at my watch shows I've been waiting almost exactly an hour when my rescuer beckons me outside. I pack my laptop back into the bag and follow him to where my car is now running perfectly.

"There you go sweetheart, all fine now."

He hands me a bill.

"£2000? How on earth can it cost that much for an hour's work?"

"'Fraid it needed a new engine, love. I haven't charged you for the tow, seeings as I was on my way to work anyway."

I notice he's removed his nasty suit and is dressed in

overalls and sweating as though he's been working hard.

"You work here?"

"I'm the owner, Patrick Spink."

"So, Mr Spink, you've replaced the engine on this car," I rest my bag on my car bonnet and turn to face him. "You've done the job in less than an hour and you're charging me £2000?"

"That's right, love. Your lucky day breaking down where I happened to be passing."

"Yes, you're right. I've only been in my job a couple of weeks and already I've got a scoop."

"What you on about, girlie?" If anything, he's looking even hotter now.

"Replacing an engine takes considerably longer than an hour. That's not including the time it takes to get hold of one and I happen to know they stopped making new engines for this model eight years ago."

"You know a lot about cars all of a sudden."

"I'm working as a researcher for a new TV programme exposing garages that take advantage of women drivers. This bag contains a video camera."

Mr Spink is crying as I hand him my card.

I call over one of the mechanics. "You'd better see to your boss, I think he's having some kind of breakdown."

17. Motivating Your Team

Christy checked her son's trousers before throwing them into the wash. Four coins, two sweet wrappers and a letter from the school addressed to her asking her to bake cakes for sports day. The sports day which was cancelled due to rain. Surely she'd washed his trousers since then?

It was a struggle getting him to bring them downstairs and she refused to wash them unless he did. At twelve years old he was quite capable of realising when his clothes needed to be washed and leaving them ready for her to do. Still he'd done it this weekend, without a single nag from her. Maybe she'd got him trained at last?

Liam wandered into the kitchen. "Oh you found the note. Sorry, forgot to give it to you before."

"Oh well, as the sports day was cancelled I don't suppose it matters."

"Not cancelled, Mum. Postponed. It's on Friday now."

"Which Friday?"

"The one that comes after Thursday."

Resisting the urge to point out his sarcastic communication method was not an effective way of influencing her, Christy read the letter again. Sure enough sports day was the coming week.

"Liam! Why do you keep doing this? You know I need notice for these things."

"Don't sweat it, Mum. Just buy some cakes and mess up the icing a bit so they look homemade. That's what most mums do."

Christy almost regretted giving him the notes from the assertiveness course she'd done recently. It might have helped him at school but it hadn't helped her much at home.

"The cakes aren't the issue, Liam. The problem is you didn't tell me sports day had been re-arranged; I'm working all next week."

"You're the boss. Take a day off."

"I'm a manager of one small section, not the boss and no, I can't just take the day off as I'm on a course all week."

"You'll think of something, Mum."

She appreciated his faith in her and wished it were justified. The worst of it was that the course would largely be a waste of time. Half a morning would be spent explaining the purpose of the course, which the delegates had already worked out from the title. More time would be lost telling them what they would learn in the next section and recaps of what they'd covered in the last. Then there were the ghastly 'ice breaking sessions' where you introduce the person next to you. The only reason people were so tense was the knowledge they'd have to do that. It was particularly embarrassing when you worked with them or knew them from all the other courses you'd attended. Christy hadn't ever come across a person who couldn't concentrate on a course because they were wondering how many children and/or pets other delegates had, whether or not they'd tried skydiving and what they felt to be their greatest achievement (which was usually to do with children, pets or skydiving).

Half the course involved the instructor reading words displayed on a powerpoint presentation, even though everyone could have read it more quickly themselves, but didn't need to as they'd be given the whole thing as a handout to take home. The other half involved getting into groups to discuss the points they'd been presented with but hadn't really followed due to dozing in the stuffy lecture room. One person from each group always nipped out for a smoke or urgent phone call leaving the rest to gossip as they waited, then quickly scribble the few key words they remembered from the last session.

"What's for tea, Mum?" Liam interrupted her thoughts.

"Whatever you like… provided every plate, cup and fork that you've taken to your room this week is clean and in the cupboard when I start cooking."

His expression looked just like a course delegate who'd been told, 'And now we're going to do a fun syndicate exercise!'

Tedious, that's what most courses were after you'd done two or three. It wasn't that she thought what they were taught was unimportant. Christy was all for health and safety, equal opportunities and all the rest of it, she just wasn't sure these messages were being conveyed as effectively as possible. She should know, her last course was 'working effectively'.

Christy was tempted to just phone in sick on the Friday, but she couldn't do that, even though Liam was now washing up, and witnessing that probably counted as a shock to her nervous system. She was a manager and the course was 'Motivating Your Team'. What sort of example would she set by not bothering to go, even if the last day was the most pointless of all. Delegates would be invited to ask questions. Nobody would because they wanted to go home. There would be a questionnaire on how good the course was or wasn't. Everyone would tick 'acceptable' or better as anything less else required them to explain the problem. Then they'd have to hang around while a certificate they didn't want was printed.

She reckoned that if the introductions and ice breakers were skipped, people read the notes for themselves, while they had their coffees and the instructor printed certificates, and the chatting sessions were combined with lunch, the course could be over a day early. That would still allow time for a proper question and question and answer session on Thursday morning while people were awake and relatively interested, for a quick test everyone really had understood the key points and for the instructor to get great feedback in the questionnaire at the end.

The washing machine beeped.

"Shall I put that on the airer, Mum?" Liam asked.

"Thanks, love." What did he want? "Everything all right, love?"

"Uh, yeah… uh, I invited Toby for tea and sort of forgot to tell you. He'll be here in a minute."

"Ah. Shall I grab a couple of pizzas from the freezer and squash them so they look home made?"

He grinned. "You're a fast learner! And you're really good at making banana splits, just saying." He hauled the wet clothes from the machine.

As she made the boys their tea, Christy thought she'd learned a lot about motivation from her son. Perhaps she could pass that on to her team?

On Monday morning Christy walked into the classroom and looked around her. Toby's mum was there, presumably her son was no better at passing on notes than Liam. The woman didn't look any happier at the thought of a whole week in the classroom than Christy felt. Looking at the other delegates Christy realised that although there had been a couple of names on the attendance list she'd not immediately been able to place she already knew everyone at least as well as she would after an introduction from their neighbour.

She took a seat in the already hot and stuffy room and waited for everyone to arrive.

The course began with the usual stuff about toilets and fire evacuation procedures, but the next bit wasn't what the delegates had been expecting.

"One way of motivating people is to find out what they want and help them achieve it in return for their co-operation in getting what you want, so please raise your hand if you'd like Friday off."

Everyone, Christy included, raised their hand. She thought Toby's mum winked at her.

"Good, well I have a plan …"

Christy's plan was eagerly accepted by all the delegates on the course she was instructing, especially Toby's mum.

"Thanks so much, Christy. A brilliant course and I feel really motivated… to buy you tea and cake at the sports day, if you'll let me?"

18. Final Act

Martin watched Lord Bingley-Smythe stride down the street as though he owned it; which he did.

The lord glanced at his reflection in one of the glass fronted premises. Clearly that's what he was doing; he was too old for space hoppers, and had no children. No family at all.

He was too old for the latest fashions too. There should be a law against anyone over twenty-five wearing flares and having ridiculously long, curly hair. But laws took no account of Martin's wishes. They were made by, and for, the rich and powerful. People like Lord Bingley-Smythe.

He was good looking in a way, Martin grudgingly admitted. Clothes maketh the man and Lord B-S spent enough on his. Didn't get them from charity shops like Martin had to. Not that expensive tailoring could ever make Martin look good. No suit, however wide the trousers, could disguise his wasted leg. No shoes, however much extra leather was added to the cuban heel of the right, could prevent his limp.

Martin didn't envy the other man for what he couldn't have. Better instead to get from him what he could; his money. Martin's money really, morally at least. Lord Bingley-Smythe wasn't quite what he seemed. Neither was Martin.

He waited impatiently for his enemy to approach. "Your Lordship," he said.

The lord frowned. "Oh, hello."

Martin introduced himself.

The lord didn't react to Martin's name, but held out a hand. "Nice to meet you, Mr Standish."

Martin placed his withered hand in the soft, healthy one. The lord didn't react to that either, but as his gaze met Martin's he dropped his arm and took a step back. "Is there something I can do for you, Mr Standish?"

"As it happens there is." Martin gave a smile which wasn't returned. It wasn't that sort of smile.

"Go on," the lord encouraged.

"You're a patron of the arts, I believe?"

"Sometimes. If a project interests me."

"What I have to say will interest you." Martin gave another grim smile.

"Are you a painter, Mr Standish? A writer?"

"A playwright." It sounded so much classier than blackmailer.

"And you want me to fund your play, is that it?" Lord B-S asked.

"It's more what you want, your Lordship. Perhaps you'd prefer to invest in it not being put on?"

"You're not making sense."

"It's a very interesting play, in that way art sometimes imitates life. It's about people. About contrasts too. Rich and poor, strong and weak, right and wrong. We can see this all around us, can we not?"

"I suppose." The lord looked bored.

"It's set in India, over forty years ago. Before Ghandi changed things."

"Really? Anywhere in particular?"

Martin named the town.

"You have my interest now, Mr Standish. I was actually born out there!"

Martin was surprised the lord admitted it. "The play shows two English families living among the natives. One rich; masters, lords even, of all they surveyed. One poor, unimportant. The rich lady and the woman who dressed her, are pregnant at same time. This was forty years ago, remember."

"Yes, go on." The lord sounded irritated. Was he beginning to guess the truth?

"The rich woman's child was sickly, not expected to live. She adopted the other baby, giving hers in exchange. The parents were given some money – and no choice."

"Extraordinary. I was adopted! I didn't find out until I was an adult."

"And what did you do?" Martin asked.

"Do about what?"

The lord knew the truth and didn't care – what had Martin expected? His rich parents rejected their crippled child, why would they bring up an adopted son to have compassion?

"You don't care at all about the other child?"

"It was sad, of course," the lord said.

It? Sad? It was a good thing Martin hadn't bought that gun or he'd have shot Lord Bingley-Smythe in the crowded street. That would have been a waste of his painstaking research. Too often Martin acted without thinking and lost an opportunity as a result. Not this time. He forced himself to speak calmly.

"The discarded child was cheated of everything. Money; for treatment that might have helped his limbs grow stronger. His family too. The other parents did what they could, but watching him suffer and trying to meet the cost of medical care, plus the heartbreak of being cheated out of their real child sent them to early graves."

"Other parents? But …" Finally the lord showed emotion. After a moment he regained his composure. "I'm sorry, Mr Standish. I was confusing your play with my own situation. I'm sure the two are very different."

Going to play the innocent was he? That didn't matter to Martin, there was only thing he was interested in. "So, you'll give me the money, your Lordship?"

"Please, there's no need to call me that. My name is Arthur."

"Well, Arthur, are you going to give me the money?"

"Yes, I'll fund your play. Do you have a script I can see?"

He was very cool! Martin handed him a large envelope. "These are copies of my research. I'll call on you in a three days so we can discuss funding and if you want to begin rehearsals or not." Martin limped away.

A car pulled up beside him. The driver leant across and opened the passenger door.

"Looks like your gammy leg is giving you trouble today."

Martin recognised the man as someone who lived near him and who often rubbed the fact that he had a car, and Martin hadn't, in his nose. "Gives me trouble every day. What's it to you?"

"I had been going to offer you a lift, but I see that as usual you prefer your own miserable company." He slammed the door and drove off.

Martin got that a lot; people showed they were easily able to help him but unless he fell about with gratitude they usually refused to do so.

Martin dragged himself up the imposing stone steps, rang the bell, and waited for the heavy oak door to open.

"Please come in, Mr Standish. Can I take your coat, get you a drink?"

"You don't have a servant to do that, your Lordship?"

"I thought we could talk more comfortably, just the two of us. And please call me Arthur."

"So you're ready to talk?"

"Indeed, I am." Lord Bingley-Smythe led him into a spacious and lavish office and gestured to a chair. "May I call you Martin?"

Martin shrugged and sat on the edge of the modern leather seat and looked around. The room was a mix of old fashioned luxury and modern convenience. Paintings, probably originals, hung on the walls. The huge antique desk held a telephone, electronic typewriter and calculator as well as a crystal ink well and pen set. The pen looked to be made of gold and matched a letter opener encrusted with glittering jewels.

Lord Bingley-Smythe leaned forward and looked Martin the eyes. "I've read your paperwork. There is no play, is there?"

"No. I'm still willing to keep quiet about everything … I imagine that's what you want?"

"Not at all. I've passed everything on to my solicitors and …"

"You what? Why?" Martin asked.

"I wanted to know the truth and I think I do. You're the boy not expected to live – but you did!"

Martin nodded.

"I'd tried tracing my birth parents when I learned of my adoption, but they'd died by then. I didn't know you hadn't. I was officially adopted. Were you?"

Martin sagged. The lord knew the truth; too much of it. As he'd discovered, legally he was entitled to the money and Martin, because of their respective adoptions, was due only one thing.

"Adopted children can't inherit titles, your lordship."

"Very true. I keep telling people not to refer to me as a lord, but no one takes any notice. Oh! I expect the title belongs to you."

Maybe it did, but being a penniless lord wasn't what he wanted. He'd now never get what should have been his by birth; respect, privilege and wealth. Instead he'd be arrested for attempted blackmail. He was weak and sickly; he'd die in prison.

"You look pale, Martin. Let me get you that drink." Arthur Bingley-Smythe moved to a small cabinet.

Martin grabbed the jewel-encrusted letter opener from the desk and stabbed the other man as he poured the finest brandy into a cut glass goblet.

The thin, strong blade slid easily through the thick woollen jacket and Arthur sank wordlessly onto the richly-coloured tapestry carpet. The only sound was the clunk as the decanter knocked the cabinet leg before landing next to the glass. Hardly a drop was spilled.

Martin snatched everything he could from the desk; gold pen, money, chequebook. He reached for the letter opener, but couldn't face pulling it from the still warm body. As he hurried out he collided with two men and landed, dazed, at the bottom of the steps.

"Mr Standish, I presume?" One said, taking Martin's elbow and helping him to his feet.

"And all ready to sign the paperwork," said the other, retrieving Arthur Bingley-Smythe's gold pen.

Martin hadn't the strength to resist as they steered him back into the office.

"Paperwork?" he mumbled.

"Lord Bingley-Smythe wishes to address the inequalities resulting from your respective adoptions. He suggests you consider yourselves brothers and the estate he's recently inherited be split between you. We're his solicitors and have come to draw up the …" The last word turned into a horrified scream.

The solicitor dropped the gold pen and knelt by the body. He felt Arthur's neck. "He's still got a pulse, call an ambulance and notify the police."

Martin stood transfixed as his colleague called. The two men then gently moved Arthur so they could loosen his cravat. As they did the weapon fell to the floor.

"It's hardly scratched him. I think he must have fainted."

Martin's head swam and his legs buckled.

When the authorities arrived they found two solicitors, two unconscious men and a great deal of incriminating paperwork.

19. Watching The Clock

Albert checked the clock. Six thirty was far too early to get up. He knew that; his wife had told him so right after his retirement. He'd woken as usual at six twenty-nine, on the following Monday, and reached to silence the alarm before it could wake Constance. For years he'd done that, usually managing to switch it off just before it emitted its shrill demand that he leave the warm comfort of his bed and begin the working day. That morning he hadn't prevented the clock making a noise, because it had never been set.

"Just you go back to sleep," she'd told him and promptly followed her own advice.

He'd wrapped himself around her; pleased to be close, unable to sleep. Each morning that week followed the same pattern. Gradually he became accustomed to retirement. Albert and Constance visited places they'd promised themselves they would see once Albert was retired. Then Constance became ill. Really ill. Everything changed then.

For the last five months, he'd not set the alarm. He had no train to catch, no meetings to attend, no in-tray awaiting his attention. There was nothing at all he must do. Nothing that couldn't be put off until tomorrow. Nobody making demands on his time. He was a man of leisure, could spend his day as he pleased, sleep as late as he liked. He still awoke at the same time every morning. Almost fifty years of routine were hard to break. At weekends, he'd always slept a little later, only a little though. Weekends had been precious. He used to love spending the time with his young wife and later their children too. When the children had grown and left, his weekends were still precious. Albert and Constance enjoyed taking day trips to museums, exhibitions, and shows or just staying at home working in the garden or reading together in companionable silence. There were visits from the children and grandchildren to look forward to. Weekends had never been long enough for all the pleasures life had to offer him. They were too short to waste on sleeping the morning away.

The days were less easy to tell apart now. There was no longer the same eagerness for Friday evenings and pang of regret on Monday mornings. Weekends were still the time he was most likely to receive visits from his family; the children still had jobs which kept them away from home. They were no longer the days in which to squeeze in a week's worth of happiness with his dear Constance.

Albert glanced at the clock again, six forty-eight. Still too early to slip out from under the quilt, pull his dressing gown on and pad barefoot downstairs to make tea. For the last forty-five years, he'd made tea in the morning for his wife and himself. For the first few years she'd made their sandwiches for work whilst he attended to breakfast. Later she was often awake earlier, the children claiming her attention. Once they'd grown she took to sleeping later and he'd taken up her tea just before leaving for work. For the first few weeks after his retirement, he'd got up first and made tea, carrying a cup to his wife.

He thought of all the hours he'd wished away during his working life. He'd been waiting for the few minutes he shared with his children after his long commute, the few wonderful hours with Constance, and the too short weekends. He'd thought his clock watching days would end when he became a pensioner, but here he was, still doing it.

Albert looked at the clock again, six fifty-seven. Still too early. He scrunched his pillow, stretched out his legs and closed his eyes. He let his mind drift back to the day he met Constance. It might not have exactly been love at first sight, but it was something pretty close. The moment he first saw her he wanted to speak to her, to know her better. They'd always been able to talk about anything, everything. When Constance collapsed, just three weeks after his retirement, he'd been at her side whispering words of love and reassurance as they waited for the ambulance. When the tests revealed there was no cure for her condition they discussed this honestly. The implications for Albert's future not ignored. Her wishes clearly expressed.

He established a new routine, arranging his day so he was by her bedside the moment the hospital allowed visitors, staying until the evening nursing staff began to look at their watches, tactfully reminding him it was time to leave. He had no reason to make those visits now; her time in a hospital bed had been mercifully brief.

A rattling sound by his ear made him glance once more towards the clock, he couldn't see it. His view was blocked by a cup of tea.

"Well, Albert, it's a long time since I was up and about before you," Constance remarked.

"Not since the boys were babies. So what's the plan for today?"

"I'll make up the picnic while you water the hanging baskets, then we'll be ready straight after my appointment with my diabetic nurse, for our trip to the gardens. I'll be glad to walk round this time rather than being pushed about in that chair like I had to be after my fall."

"I'm glad too, hard work that was."

"Cheeky! I'm only a pound or two heavier than I was on our wedding day."

"Good and I hope you can still walk briskly, because I've got a bowls match tonight."

"How could I forget that? Didn't I spend all day yesterday getting your whites clean and pressed?"

"No you did not. We looked round the art gallery half the morning, played with the grandchildren all afternoon and spent the evening at the Jones's playing bridge."

"Well, apart from those things, I spent the whole day looking after you. Now are you getting up? We've lots to do. Just look at the time."

Albert looked: nine-forty seven was far too late to still be in bed.

20. Timing

"In order to provide a safe and punctual service for all our passengers, train doors will close thirty seconds before departure. Please plan sufficient time for your journey," the announcement reminds me.

I look up at the boards to check which platform my train leaves from. I have to squint to read it from back here. If I get any closer, I risk getting bumped into by the crowds of people checking details and rushing off without a thought to the injured ribs and shoulder of the woman behind them. Platform eight in twenty minutes. Good, that gives me time to buy a book, although not long to make a selection.

As you'd expect from a WH Smith shop, there's one of those 'two for three' deals on. Of course, I buy three. The first two books are ones I've heard Justin's friends say are good. My fiancé's friends are classy; the books won't be fun, but hopefully they'll be interesting enough to occupy my mind during the journey from Waterloo to Birmingham. My final choice is one recommended by a friend at work. She said it's hilarious, so I'd better not read it yet. I could do with cheering up, but laughter will hurt.

By the simple precautions of waiting for someone else to push the button to open the door and not trying to put my bag or coat into the overhead rack, I manage to settle into my seat without adding to my pain. After an hour of reading a book described as, 'the subtle metaphor for humanity's rejection of understanding' my head is hurting as much as my bruised body. The book isn't subtle, it's totally incomprehensible.

I swallow some painkillers and decide to look at the countryside flashing by instead. There are so many shades of green. Mentally, I list as many as I can; lime, olive, mint, bay. Funny how many are types of food; or is it just that I'm hungry? I should have bought chocolate as well as books.

The trees, wild flowers and grass give way to empty ploughed fields. I give the second book a try. At least it's got a story, even if it is more 'thought provokingly intriguing' than the straightforward gripping read I'd have preferred. Two chapters in, the train slows, stops then moves forward slowly. The guard announces a fault. Another page and we stop; in a station this time.

"The train now standing at platform three is the seventeen fifty-two service for Birmingham New Street. This service will be delayed approximately twenty minutes due to a temporary fault. We apologise for the delay this will cause to your journey."

The delay isn't really going to make much difference; my parents will still be waiting to take me home. I smile as I think about them. A couple of weeks with Mum fussing over me and Dad calling me his 'little princess' are just what I need. This time a twenty minute wait isn't going to change my life.

It's all about timing isn't it? What we do, who we do it with. Because of the timing of an accident, I'm following train timetables, not checking flight times. I'll be spending my holiday with my parents in Birmingham, not my fiancé in Bern.

I stare at the book and turn pages, but I'm not reading; I'm remembering how a twenty minute wait had, eventually lead to our engagement. Justin and I had both been queuing in the chemists at the same time. The assistant serving me and the one serving him spoke almost in stereo, "That will take about twenty minutes."

He'd turned to me, "It seems we've both got a few minutes to kill, fancy joining me next door for a coffee?"

Of course coffee with a tall, tanned blue-eyed hunk had sounded far more interesting than browsing the racks of vitamins and denture cleaners and I'd agreed without hesitation. Neither had I hesitated in falling for his charming manner. He'd held open the door of the chemist and then the coffee shop, thought nothing of paying the high prices charged for our drinks and had offered me a cake too. His suit and the watch I glimpsed, as he shook my hand, looked expensive.

"I'm Justin," he said.

"Laura," I said and grasped his hand. "Don't worry, I haven't got anything contagious, the prescription is for my boss."

"Mine is for malaria tablets, I'm off to Kenya soon, for a safari. Have you ever been?"

I wasn't sure if he meant to Kenya or on a safari, but my answer was the same in either case. "I've never been abroad."

"No? Well maybe I'll… Maybe you'll get the chance soon."

Justin told me he was busy before his trip, but asked if I'd like to have lunch with him when he returned. I'd agreed, of course. He'd been even more tanned and gorgeous by then. The lunch had been in a really posh restaurant where even the starters cost over a tenner. It wasn't just his generosity that impressed me; he was attractive, clever and confident. He showed me a sophisticated and luxurious world I'd hardly realised existed.

"The train now standing at platform three is the delayed seventeen fifty-two service for Birmingham New Street. This service will depart in two minutes."

An elderly lady in a burgundy coat and matching hat makes her way down the carriage and stands, hopefully, near me. "Phew, lucky for me the train was delayed."

Funny how sometimes what seems like bad luck can be good; for some people at least. I lean forward and move my bag from the opposite seat.

"Thanks," she says as she edges past me.

Twisting to put my bag next to me causes a jolt of pain and I wince.

"Oh, sorry. Did I knock you dear? I didn't mean to." She removes her coat to reveal a skirt and waistcoat in the same deep reddish shade. I wonder what her favourite colour is?

I shoot burgundy lady a quick smile to let her know it's not her fault, but keep quiet. I want to concentrate on my book, not think about the cause of my painful ribs.

Maybe it's time now, for another dose of painkillers? I'd been hoping I could miss this dose and have a drink when I arrive. Perhaps I'd better take them; I think they're anti-inflammatory. Stupidly I didn't pay attention to the doctor. I'd been more concerned with Justin's reaction.

Of course, when I twist to reach into my bag, my ribs remind me why I'm reaching for the pills.

"Are you OK, dear?" the lady asks. Her accent is just like Mum's. I swallow the lump that forms in my throat.

"I will be once these kick in," I assure her.

"Oooh, yes. I have those when my hip plays up. Good they are."

I nod and read the label. Yes, anti-inflammatory. Gingerly, I begin to reach out towards my bag.

"Here, let me." She picks up my bag and moves it to my other side, placing it close to me.

"Thanks."

I find my water bottle without further pain and swallow two painkillers. The water is warm and not at all delicious. I check the label on the tablets again. Ah! 'May cause drowsiness; if affected do not drive or operate heavy machinery.' No mention of alcohol. That's all right then. As long as I stay awake, I can have a glass of wine down the legion with Mum and Dad. Sweet wine. For now, I make do with another swig of warm water. Maybe I'm pulling a face, because the lady produces a pack of sweets.

"Here, have one of these to take the taste away."

The bag contains cherry drops, deep red cherry drops. I smile. "I've never met anyone who chooses sweets to match their clothes, before."

"I don't always," she says laughing. "Otherwise I could never eat chocolate limes. They're scrumptious, but lime just doesn't agree with my complexion."

I look down at my own clothes; dark brown trousers, cream sweater, brown coat. "Maybe I should have brought some chocolate brazils?"

"Or truffles. I do like a nice Viennese truffle."

She tells me about a small sweet shop near where she lives, that makes all their confectionary by hand. That's where she bought the cherry drops. I agree that they taste extremely good. She offers me the bag again and explains that the makers use only natural ingredients. Another announcement drowns her out.

"A buffet trolley serving a variety of hot and cold drinks and sweet and savoury snacks operates on this train. Please keep the aisles clear."

Good, I can get a bottle of chilled water. I hear the doors hiss. Stupidly, I look round to see if the trolley is being pushed through into our compartment. Twisting is painful and I wince again.

"I hope it's nothing serious?" burgundy lady asks, once I've made my purchase.

"Just a fall," I say and try to turn my attention back to my book.

I can't concentrate. I keep remembering being sprawled in the frozen food aisle, waiting for the ambulance and trying to phone Justin. I didn't think he was particularly annoyed I couldn't go skiing; more that I'd dislocated my knee and cracked three ribs in ASDA. If it had been in a smart speciality shop, he might have been more impressed. That's harsh I realise now, but it is true that once he's made plans he expects everyone to comply with them and that he'll never know how slippery supermarket floors can be. In hospital, I had time to listen to the doubts I'd been having about our relationship.

Justin brought me flowers; a huge bouquet of lilies, roses and orchids.

"You can still come to Switzerland, Laura, even if you can't ski," he'd said. His voice was full of the concern I'd heard in the voice of the burgundy clad stranger sat opposite me now.

"Skiing, did you say? Was it a bad fall?" she asked.

I hadn't realised I'd said anything. "I didn't fall skiing. I fell over in a supermarket. I was going on a ski holiday; all those lessons on the dry ski slope are wasted now."

"You fell in the supermarket?"

"Yes, that's right; I'd taken skiing lessons and yet had my accident in the supermarket." I chuckle, it does sound silly.

I couldn't share that bit of irony with Justin. He doesn't know I can't ski. There are other things he doesn't know about me. He doesn't know I prefer sweet wine to the dry, oaked chardonnay he drinks. He doesn't know I prefer Maeve Binchey to those clever books his friends keep recommending. He doesn't know because I've never let him see the real me.

My new friend smiles. "It's good that you can see the funny side of it. It seems like rotten timing, but I'm sure you'll get better and be back to your old self soon."

"The next station stop is Coventry. Coventry the next stop."

"Gracious! This is me." She's doing her coat up as she speaks. "The time has just flown by whilst we've been chatting."

We say goodbye and she's soon gone, pulling on her burgundy hat as she heads for the exit.

'Rotten timing' she'd said. Well, yes it should have been, Justin and I had just got engaged. I'd worked hard to fit in with his crowd. When I was invited to join their skiing party, I was pleased, although it wouldn't have been much of a holiday for me. I'd have had to spend the fortnight maintaining the image I'd created for myself. Now I'm looking forward to relaxing and having time to just be me.

Justin was invited to Birmingham too, but it's not really

his scene, just like his life isn't mine. Burgundy lady said she hoped I'd get back to my old self soon. I hope so too.

"The next station stop is Birmingham New Street. This train terminates here. Please ensure you take all personal belongings with you when you depart the train. We wish you a pleasant onward journey."

The end of the line. I'll have to tell Justin it's over. Not whilst he's on holiday, but soon; before he starts making plans for the wedding. I'll find the right moment; timing is everything.

21. Safe As Houses

Number 27 Hawthorn Crescent is, I suppose, not much of a house, but there's no chain and the asking price is surprisingly low. A glance at the glossy sheet of paper, supplied by the estate agency, makes the property sound enticing. It lists reception rooms, a modern kitchen and bathroom, enclosed garden, master and guest bedrooms, a wealth of period detail, full central heating and double glazing throughout. The photograph, however, reveals the truth; the shabby terrace is just a few tiny rooms squeezed between its grander neighbours.

"We'll meet at the house at six, if that's OK?" Jemima the estate agent had said.

"That's a bit early," I told her. Occasionally, I'm asked to stay at work an extra half hour to get something finished. Doing overtime is the only way I can afford even the most modest house.

"Six thirty?" she asked.

"I should be able to get there for then," I replied. "I don't want to keep anyone waiting though …"

"Don't worry, Jo. I've got a key so we can just go straight in."

She must have sensed how nervous I was.

"Look, really there's nothing to worry about. I realise this is your first time, and that it's a big step, but try to relax and leave everything to me. This is my job, I'll help you. You don't have to make a decision straight away, let's just see how things go shall we?"

Of course it's her job to build up trust and confidence and she did it so well. Her slick manner and slick suit are simply an extension of her slick 'been there done that' attitude. I began to believe that the buying and selling of houses is just an everyday business deal, not a make or break life changing decision.

All day at work, I haven't been able to concentrate. Should I go through with this? Was I making a huge mistake? Although I had been saving for our own home with my fiancé, I'd never lived anywhere other than my parents' home. We all thought I would be married and settled by now. I'm sure they were looking forward to some time alone together, but when Danny dumped me, they had offered to continue to provide me with a home.

"You can stay with us as long as you like, Jo love," they had promised, despite the disruption that my acceptance might cause to their own plans.

It would be comforting to continue to live with them. I felt safe with them, to live alone would seem strange, almost dangerous, but I have to grow up sometime. Is now really the right time to move away? Yes; the engagement has been broken, but not my determination to set up home independently of my family. Besides when am I ever going to find another house in my price range? I finish work and race to Hawthorn Crescent.

I arrive at six thirty-one, just in time to see Jemima disappear through the front door.

"This is Paul and Louise Ashby," she introduces the couple standing in the hallway. "Jo Chambers," she gestures toward me.

We all shake hands.

"Shall we start?" Jemima asks.

I nod my agreement and we begin the tour.

"The kitchen is only a little over a year old and the bathroom has been re-done recently," Jemima informs her audience.

We look at the stylish modern fittings. Everything fits perfectly into this old building. I don't have to be told about the original features I can see them for myself. I don't need to be told about the character, charm and atmosphere, I can feel it flowing round me the way a cat weaves its way about your legs.

"The owners are retiring to Portugal, they need a quick sale, that's why the price is so reasonable," Jemima explains. "The interior, as you can see, is beautifully maintained."

She is right, clever attention to detail has made the most of the limited space. Everything is well cared for and nicely decorated. The outside is a different matter.

"The exterior just needs a lick of paint, to bring it up to the same high standard as the surrounding properties. Everything is structurally sound," Jemima assures us.

She is right I realise.

"Perhaps you'd like to see the garden?" she asks as she unlatches the French windows and steps into the cramped courtyard.

"This intimate space is ideal for eating al fresco and beautifully easy to maintain."

As she speaks, I imagine pots of bright flowers, a table, chairs, a bottle of wine, maybe a man to share it with.

Jemima ushers us upstairs. I glance out of the window to what at first appears to be a dull view. Jemima soon points out that it is tranquil and relaxing. The rooms aren't small, they're compact. This isn't simply the scruffiest house in the street, it's full of potential, located in a sought after area. The house isn't packed into a heavily built up area with neighbours crowding in on all sides, it is conveniently placed next to local amenities. This isn't an anonymous busy part of town, this is a bustling friendly community. This is a place where I can, once again, be happy.

"I'm sorry, Jemima, Mr and Mrs Ashby, I can't go through with it," I say.

Jemima stares at me; she must have thought this deal was as safe as the houses she sells.

"Sorry," I say again. "I just can't sell my parents' house and follow them to Portugal. It's my home and I'm going to stay here."

22. Last Obsession

I'd better buy a green pen. That'd definitely help. Green's a lucky colour, everyone knows that. The bookies know for sure, that's why those little ones they provide are always blue or red. Well, they don't want to help you win, stands to reason. Can't really blame them can you? They've got a business to run after all.

I've got the green pen now. A real good one it is too. Cost £20. The missus was none too pleased. Said we could've used that money for something more important. Like the mortgage I suppose. Shows what she knows. We're so far behind with that a score's not going to make a difference. Women don't understand finance. She said to pay some was better than none. Would show good faith she said. Well, when I've got my system running I'll pay it all off, what we owe and the rest. That'll show them a lot more than good faith. No more mortgage. No more nagging. No more sarcastic letters wondering if we're having trouble meeting the payments and perhaps we'd like to come in to 'discuss the matter further'.

This pen's an investment. Tried to explain that to the little woman, but she didn't get it. I love her, but sometimes she's a worry to me. I want her to be happy; I just don't know how to explain to her that it's all going to work out.

"It's not a toy for me," I told her. "It's for us, for our future."

"What, to sign the bankruptcy papers with?"

"To work out my system," I explain. Women don't understand gambling either. "Loads of people make a packet this way," I reasoned "People wouldn't do it otherwise."

"Yeah and loads of people don't. That's why it's called gambling."

"It's only gambling when you don't know what you're doing."

"And you do?"

"I've almost got it figured." I nipped down the bookies quick. I could see there was going to be an argument if I stayed in.

I just put £50 on the last race and lost of course. Would have, wouldn't I? Too cautious, that's my trouble. Too worried about what the wife will have to say, and the money we owe.

She's pregnant. That makes a difference; my luck needs to change fast, if I'm to provide for the little one. My mind wasn't on the matter in hand. No one can win like that.

She won't let me get a decent stake together. Seems like she don't have a lot of faith in me. Be all smiles and, 'Oh well done darling, you were lucky,' when I win though won't it? Luck, huh! Well, you make your own luck don't you?

Just heard about a dead cert. Old Mac told me; it can't fail. He gave me a tip like this before, it won and I only had a pittance on it. I won't make that mistake again. Went to draw out our savings. They're all gone. To pay for food, electricity, insurance, things like that she said. Stupid woman. Does she never think ahead?

I took the jewellery her mother gave her. The TV and video too. They're rented so I won't get much for them, but I know a place that'll give cash no questions asked. I even managed to get a couple of quid for the bottles of drink left over from Christmas. She thinks I don't have any initiative; that I won't put in the effort to get a job done. Well, she's wrong isn't she? OK, So I'm not great at stuff round the house and those two bit agency jobs aren't worth breaking your back over. Thing is I can do it, when it's important. Managed to open the electric meter didn't I? £25 I got, well almost. £25 on electricity! What was she thinking? No sense of priorities at all.

Exactly £357 I managed to get together. I put the lot on, no messing. 16-1 it was. £5712 I'd get back before tax. Check on a calculator if you don't believe me. Good at maths I am. Have to be in this game don't you? I'm not stupid either. I know that much money isn't enough to set us up for life. It's enough to get me started. A stake like that and I could afford to take a few risks. I'd back the outsiders, only when I knew I was on to a good thing, of course. That's the way to make real money. Backing the favourite never made anyone rich.

Watched the race down the Black Horse. Told the landlord that my luck had changed at last, so he let me have a pint on the slate until I collected my winnings. Last Obsession is a black horse I notice as they parade him round. That could be coincidence of course; there's lots of black horses. But it could be a lucky omen. The jockeys come out to mount. There's one in green silk, is he the one? He is, he is. Definitely an omen. The horse takes the lead at the first. He increases it at the third. He maintains it 'til the one before last. It's neck and neck around the bend.

He falls at the last.

I realise where I've been going wrong. I've been messing around up to now. The winnings haven't come because the stakes haven't been high enough. She's been raising the stake with them insurance premiums for years. Well, I'll gamble everything and win it all back for her and the baby. Maybe she did plan ahead. Perhaps she'll understand. I'll go over to that fancy new tower block with the stockbrokers and financial consultants. I'll go up to the twelfth floor, that's high enough.

I'll jump from there.

23. Cedric's Last Meal

The box was outside the charity shop when I came to unlock this morning. I took a quick glance inside, spotted what appeared to be an urn and closed the flap quickly. I thought the shock of Cedric's death was making me hallucinate.

I made a cup of tea before looking in the box again. Inside there really was an urn and it wasn't empty. There was a plaque on the side. I read Cedric's name and dates before dropping the urn. The lid stayed on. It was me, not the ashes, which fell to the ground.

"Emily, what on earth's wrong?" Millie asked as soon as she arrived.

I showed her the vase.

"That's the name of your friend's husband isn't it? But, that can't be right. I thought the cremation wasn't until tomorrow."

"So did I."

"What are you doing with an urn anyway?" she asked.

"It was left outside the shop."

"Well, that's not right."

Nothing about this was right. I phoned Margaret.

"Oh hello, Emily. Got my little gift did you?"

"Why did you send it, Margaret?"

"Why not? I wasn't keen on him cluttering up my lounge when he was alive and paying the bills. I certainly don't want him doing it now."

"How can you say such a thing?" I asked.

"What's up? Don't like people talking ill of the dead? Well I don't like people lying and cheating."

"You know?"

"Oh yes, I know. I suppose it's partly my own fault, I shouldn't have donated things so generously. I didn't know you'd take my husband along with the other bric-a-brac."

"It was Cedric who donated everything, not you."

"Is that what he told you, dear? I'm sorry, but adulterous men are rather prone to lying."

"But … the urn …?"

"I just thought you'd like to have him to yourself for a change. He's no use to me now. All I need is the insurance money."

"But it's not really him. The funeral isn't until tomorrow."

"Thought it best to have it as soon as possible, to save any embarrassment."

"What embarrassment?"

The only reply was Margaret's laugh.

Why would she want to rush the funeral, unless she had something to hide? I recalled the evening Cedric died and realised the awful truth; after he'd staggered home from my house, Margaret had killed him. She'd cremated him so there was no evidence.

"It was you. You killed him! You're evil."

"Positively poisonous, Emily dear. But don't worry, I'll be moving away soon. You'll never have to see me again." She laughed again before hanging up.

Poison, she must have poisoned him I reasoned. He was

always telling me about the pills and potions she made him take. He'd said they did more harm than good, but I hadn't taken any notice.

I couldn't let her get away with it, so I told the police everything. I'm not sure they believed me to start with. They got interested when I explained about the urn. After that, they wrote down every word and I signed a statement. As I was leaving, I remembered his donor card.

"He asked for his organs to be used, will you be able to test those for poison?"

"We'll look into that, madam. Don't you worry."

They took my details and promised they would be in touch. I went straight round to confront Margaret. She didn't seem surprised.

"Come and sit down. Would you like tea?"

"No, I'm not falling for that, you'll poison me too. It was poison, wasn't it?"

"In a way. Now either come in and sit down, or go away. I refuse to argue with you on my doorstep."

I remembered what she'd said about leaving soon and decided to keep her talking so she couldn't get away before the police arrived.

"Sure you won't have some tea? I'm going to."

I refused and waited in her lounge, thinking about Cedric and all the things he'd missed and would never now have a chance to experience. We'd planned to take a trip together; he hadn't travelled much because of Margaret's fear of flying.

There was a photograph of them on the mantelpiece. As I looked at his awful comb-over I remembered how I'd teased him about it when our relationship first began. I was horrified to learn that he'd done it because of Margaret. She'd belittled him for his bald patch and insisted he cover it. I think it was after I'd assured him that his thinning and greying hair was a sign of maturity, not weakness, that he really began to care about me.

Margaret carried her drink in with a plate of biscuits. She offered me those, but obviously I didn't touch them. When she left them too, I realised I'd been right.

"So what have you come to say?" she asked. "You had an affair with my husband, don't you think you've caused me enough trouble?"

I did feel guilty about deceiving her and decided I'd done enough of that.

"Margaret, I've been to the police."

"How interesting."

"I told them everything."

"Everything, Emily?"

"How can you be so calm? Yes, I've told them everything."

"Did you tell them that you had Cedric's ashes?"

"I showed them, they've kept them as evidence."

"Good."

"I still don't understand why you sent them," I said.

"It was silly, but I thought it would make you happy to have them for a while, so you could grieve properly."

"Why would you want me to be happy? You didn't let Cedric have anything he wanted. You did your best to humiliate him. Why would you care about me?"

"Oh, you are mixed up. I don't care about you, I just felt that I owed you something."

"After what I did to you?"

"More because of what I've done to you."

"Because you made the man I loved miserable and then killed him?"

"How did I make him miserable?"

"You were too controlling."

"Oh, Emily I've told you before that cheating men lie. I didn't control him, I'd long ago realised I had no say in what he did. He just used me as an excuse when his lady friends got too demanding or he didn't want to take them somewhere. He did that with all his other women. I expect he got so used to his lies it was hard to stop telling them."

"There were no other women. He was faithful to you, until he fell in love with me. He didn't want to cheat, but he couldn't help it."

"Really, you do amuse me. How else did I mistreat him?"

"You didn't let him spend any of his money."

"Cedric was too mean to spend money on anyone. He spent it on cruises. We spent a fortune on holidays because he couldn't get up the nerve to get on a plane. He'd spend it on himself too, those ridiculously tight trousers and the leather jackets so that he could kid himself he was still trendy. And that ridiculous comb-over. Really dear, I don't know how you could stand that."

I was too surprised to reply to that. She'd forced Cedric to dress as though suffering a midlife crisis and here she was, blaming him!

"He had his own bank account and I never saw the statements. I'm afraid he just didn't want to give you gifts or pay for meals out."

"It wasn't that. He loved my cooking. He could only eat

the plainest foods because of all your allergies and dislikes, but gradually I was getting him to try new things."

"My allergies?"

"Yes, you'd made such a fuss about them he was almost paranoid. He carried your spare epipen everywhere because he was so worried you'd have an attack. He even described the symptoms to me and explained how to use it."

"Really, how thoughtful of him. I suppose he told you I won't eat spicy food too?"

"That's right. He showed me the cook book he'd bought, hoping you'd learn to be a bit more adventurous. You insisted he got rid of it, so I bought it. I saw he'd marked a page and so I cooked the recipe for him." I had to stop to blow my nose at this point. "It was his last meal before he died."

"Did you tell the police about your last evening together?" Margaret asked.

"Yes, I told them everything. How he seemed nervous when he arrived, he kept patting his pockets and seemed reluctant to eat anything. I realise now that you must have poisoned him before he came out and he was feeling ill. After just a few mouthfuls of the chicken satay, he'd complained that his lips were burning. Poor man, he was so used to the bland food you gave him that even a mildly spiced dish seemed hot to him."

"What happened then?"

"He started to look ill; he Twas anxious and not really making sense. He asked what was in the sauce. When I said not to worry, it was mainly chicken and peanuts with hardly any spice he became distressed and began mumbling about you. He left …and he died that night. I should have realised as soon as he was dead that you'd killed him. I let him come home to die, it's all my fault."

"Ys it is, but you shouldn't blame yourself. You weren't to know."

"Why did he have to die?"

"I realised you were in love with him. I thought if you insisted he leave me, he might do it. Cedric was always such a weak man. I didn't want him, but I did want his money. I was worried he'd divorce me and I'd lose the house."

"You killed him for the house?"

"Don't be silly. I didn't kill him."

"Liar."

"Yes, I have told lies, although not as many as Cedric. I'll be honest with you now. After I left his urn outside your shop, I called the police and said it had been stolen. I told them that I thought you'd killed him. I suggested they test the organs that were removed for donation."

"They'll prove you killed him."

"Not me, Emily. Are you sure you won't have one of these biscuits? They are rather good."

I looked more closely and could see that they contained peanuts. I remembered Cedric telling me that just a small amount would kill her within hours and knew she was trying to commit suicide. I watched as she took a bite. I wanted to stop her, but she'd killed before, perhaps if not herself it would be me next.

She took another bite.

"You know, Emily, if I had a peanut allergy then by now my mouth would begin to burn. Gradually my lips and throat would swell. I'd need antihistamine, just like the epipen Cedric couldn't find before his last meal, to reduce the swelling. Otherwise, it would just get worse until I couldn't breathe." She took another bite. "My lips aren't burning. Cedric's were, weren't they?"

"But that means …"

"That's right. I didn't kill him; you did."

24. Milk Bottles On The Doorstep

Fred missed his army days. Some of the lads used to grumble the army was little better than prison, but Fred hadn't agreed. Back then he always had plenty to eat and something useful to do. He could still remember his sergeant saying, 'Look lively lad, there's work to be done before you get to your dinner.' Fred had done the work, whatever was asked of him. Then he'd eaten his dinner, whatever was on offer. Lovely grub it had been too. Steak and kidney pies or chicken stew with dumplings that stuck to your ribs. Puddings too, jam tart or fruit crumble and always lashings of thick custard. Plenty of mates to chat with as you worked, or ate, or sometimes went down the pub for a couple. Good times.

Nowadays Fred was no longer a lad and he had no mates around him. It felt like he was the only one left, although he guessed some of the others must still be alive. He hoped, if they were, they lived with families or in a nice retirement home somewhere with meals laid on and people to help organise their days. Fred did his best on his own. Kept himself and the house neat and clean, but it was hard to make the effort when he often felt tired and there was nobody to see the results.

Meals were more of a problem. He wasn't much of a cook and he couldn't afford to waste food by spoiling it.

His mind was still as active as ever though, even if he was a bit forgetful. He still had some of the skills he'd learnt in the army. Those reconnoitre sorties he'd been on, the months he'd spent in the QM's department, his ability to move stealthily and act unseen. Fred worked out his campaign and put it into action.

First he located an opportunity. Not easy as few people still had their milk delivered. Including Fred, there were just three on his street of over forty houses. Fred set out early – before the milkman. Early starts and being where he was supposed to be, right when he was supposed to be there, were habits he'd picked up in the army and never abandoned.

Quiet as he could, he crept up the path of the house right at the end of his road and left a note on the doorstep. '1 extra pint today, please.' Then he hid and waited. When the milkman delivered, Fred took the surplus pint and snuck off home.

Later that morning, Fred bought a pack of jam tarts and a tin of custard powder. The girl in the corner shop might have a funny accent, but that didn't mean he couldn't understand the instructions for custard making she willingly gave. The meal wasn't quite as good as the ones he remembered, but the hot pudding was a welcome addition to his usual cheese sandwiches.

He didn't feel so tired the rest of the day. A bit more food was just what the doctor ordered, or at least might have been if Fred had gone in the surgery and bothered him. Fred had dizzy spells sometimes, but he didn't need some lad, fresh out of college with his shiny new stethoscope, telling Fred he was getting on a bit and shouldn't expect to feel as fit as he had in the army.

Fred got braver. He paid close attention to the foodstuffs the milkman supplied and, the following week, placed orders for eggs, bacon and mushrooms at three separate houses in the local area. He made himself a pretty good fry up from that lot for his tea and there was plenty left over for a couple of breakfasts later in the week. Fred felt marvellous. A few days later, he went a bit further from home and got orange juice and extra milk. By never using the same address twice, Fred hoped the people living there wouldn't be accused of theft.

He wouldn't get away with it for long, he knew. The milkman would soon be suspicious and would recognise his handwriting. Fred wandered the local streets wondering how else he could get hold of decent food. He walked down a street of detached houses. Each had a shiny car or two on the driveway and one of those dish things up on the roof. The people there probably wouldn't even notice a few pounds extra on their bills and could easily afford it if they did. Maybe he'd do one last big raid, get himself some meat and perhaps a pot of cream to go on his lunchtime bread and jam. He did, but then decided he should quit for a while.

Cheap white bread and whatever cheese was reduced because the sell-by date was fast approaching tasted even worse than he remembered after his short taste of better living. Again, Fred left his house, hoping an opportunity would present itself.

"Hi, Fred," his neighbour called. "You, OK?"

"Yes, thank you. All tickety boo!" Fred replied.

His neighbours were kind, all of them. Sometimes he'd been tempted to tell them how lonely he was, how hungry, but he had his pride. He'd never once put out one of his little notes at a house where the owner said 'good morning' to Fred, or waved as he passed.

"And you? You all right?" Fred asked.

"Couldn't be better. I'm off on holiday tomorrow. A cruise.

Six weeks of luxury, can you believe it?"

Fred couldn't. At least, he couldn't believe his unemployed neighbour could pay for such a trip. He was so surprised he actually said as much.

"I've been saving up my disability allowance for ages," the man said.

Disability? There were people who had trouble getting about and working who needed the benefits, but his neighbour surely wasn't one of them. Nor did it seem likely he had one of those invisible disabilities. Yesterday he'd been out cutting the grass, last week he'd been up a ladder adjusting his ugly plastic dish. He played football every Sunday for goodness sake!

Fred, with his arthritis and the pains in his hip when the weather turned as cold as it was now, was far more disabled than this young chap, yet he'd never had the brass neck to expect hand outs.

"I had no idea you were disabled." Fred didn't hide the scepticism he felt.

"Well, bad back I've got sometimes, haven't I?" the neighbour said.

"Right," said Fred. He was too angry to say more.

"Well, can't stop chatting, I've the packing to finish, but I wondered if you could do me a favour?"

"Oh?" Did he want the shirt off Fred's back, to protect him from the sun?

"I wondered if you could tell the milkman and pay my bill?" He disappeared inside without waiting for a reply.

Fred was still stood staring after him when the man returned with cash, lots of it.

"I feel much better giving it to you than leaving it in an

envelope. There are some right crooks about. There you go, forty-four pounds eighty, I owe him." He handed Fred forty-five pounds. "Tell him to keep the change."

"Over forty pounds on milk?" Fred asked, a feeling of guilt sweeping over him. Surely the milkman hadn't needed to increase prices so much to make up for what he'd taken?

The man laughed. "No, no. I treated myself and the wife to a bit of steak and some strawberries. Thought I should get in training for the cruise."

Fred didn't reply. He couldn't. All he could do was wonder how much his neighbour would pay in tips at the end of his luxury holiday.

Next morning, Fred was up bright and early to greet the milkman. "My neighbour asked me to give you this," Fred said. He handed over five pounds. "He said he owes you four pounds eighty and you're to keep the change."

"Four pounds … He's made a mistake, or someone has," the milkman said.

"Oh?" Fred wasn't surprised. He made mistakes like that sometimes, because of his bad memory.

"Don't worry about it, Fred. I'll sort it out with him next week."

"Yes, er …"

"What's up, Fred."

"If he's not paid enough it don't seem right to ask …"

"Ask what?"

"He wanted you to leave him some steak tomorrow and an extra pint of milk and, do you sell treacle tarts?"

"I do, yes. And he definitely asked for this? Didn't just leave a note?"

"No, no note. Why?"

"Something odd's been going on, but don't worry. Didn't ask for strawberries as well, did he?"

"Oh no. He's allergic."

Fred paid for the steak, and treacle tart with his neighbour's money the following week, saying quite truthfully that the man had given the cash to Fred to pay for his bill.

"And he said can you leave one pint of milk every day for the next five weeks and a treacle tart every Friday."

"Sure thing, Fred. I'll pass the message on."

Fred frowned.

"Didn't I say? A new chap is taking over the round."

Fred probably had known. He'd forgotten that was all. This was good news though, Fred could start out with his notes all over again.

The new milkman wasn't the good news Fred had expected him to be. He delivered later in the day. That was a problem because it meant Fred couldn't go out just before him to leave the notes and hide to retrieve the food. At six in the morning that had been easy, at half past eight, he was bound to be spotted.

Worse still, he couldn't even collect the milk from his neighbour's doorstep. The bottles sat there going sour, while Fred eked out his milk in almost black cups of tea. It wasn't right.

The new milkman seemed to agree with Fred. On the third day he banged loudly on the neighbour's door. The police were there not thirty minutes later. Fred knew what he had to do. He went out and confessed.

"It was me. I did it."

As the policeman asked him to, "Say that again," Fred felt dizzy. His vision blurred, then he collapsed.

Fred was so weak with cold and hunger he was taken to the police station, examined by a doctor and given food before anyone even began to question him. Even then, they sat him in a warm room and brought him a cup of tea. They carefully explained his rights before asking him why he'd done it.

"He's been claiming benefits he'd no right to and living in luxury while I've been cold and hungry. I know I shouldn't have done none of the the things I did, but I were that hungry …"

The policeman seemed sympathetic and Fred felt sure someone would now check up on his neighbour, so once he got back from his cruise he wouldn't be getting away with anything else.

"Tell us, Fred what did you do with the body?"

He almost collapsed again when he realised they'd assumed his brief confession was for murder, not theft.

"I'm not prepared to say," he told them. They couldn't make him, he had rights.

"How did you do it?" the officer asked.

"I don't remember." Well, he did forget things sometimes and he certainly couldn't remember using violence against his neighbour. Wouldn't hurt for the police to see he was a confused old man, Fred thought.

"We can't let you go, Fred, not if you're accused of murder," the officer told him. "You'll have to be put on remand while it's looked into."

Fred wasn't sure they really believed he was a killer, but he understood they had to keep him in until they either learned the truth or took him to court.

The prison was lovely and warm. There was plenty of food, people to talk to, they even did his laundry for him. It'd come to an end when his neighbour came back, but Fred might have worked out a plan by then. Even if he hadn't, he still had a whole month of luxury before him. Fred could hardly believe his luck.

25. Maybe Next Time

"Come on, fair's fair, we've all taken Mrs Geere at least twice, let Davey have a go," the boss of the driving test centre said.

Davey was immediately suspicious. His colleagues had pretended reluctance for him to take particular candidates before. On his first day there was a George who dressed as a flamboyant Georgina, except for size eleven work boots.

"Sorry about the strange outfit, mate. Can't brake properly in stilettos," he'd explained.

George passed his test, unlike the lady who smelled of cats and threatened to hex him. Then there was the chap with the tin foil hat. His driving wasn't too bad, but Davey doubted he was safe out on his own, with or without a car.

"How many tests has Mrs Geere failed?"

"Dozens, lad. Still she might pass today … or maybe next time."

Davey's colleagues all laughed at that. He wished he knew why. Was it to do with Mrs Geere's driving style or some local joke the new boy wouldn't understand? Oh well he'd find out soon enough, her test was scheduled just before his lunch break.

Mrs Geere looked all right. Not young by any means, but she seemed alert and sensible; she reminded him of his gran. Anyone who could lug round a handbag that size was likely to have sufficient strength to handle the wheel and operate the controls too, he reasoned.

There were no problems with her eyesight or paperwork. She pulled away perfectly, followed his directions and did a neat three point turn when requested. She showed no trace of even minor problems anywhere during the first fifteen minutes.

"Please take the next turning on the left."

Mrs Geere turned right. That wasn't an issue as she indicated and manoeuvred correctly. What mattered was how she drove, not whether nerves meant she confused left and right.

"Please take the next right."

Mrs Geere made a textbook left turn.

As Davey wanted her to take the next right he asked her to turn left.

She did.

Was she doing it on purpose? She had a rather determined expression, but then so did a lot of people when taking their driving test. She hadn't had it earlier though.

"Next left, please." It wasn't a roundabout or T junction just a single turning off the road they were on, so she couldn't possibly go the wrong way.

Mrs Geere checked her mirror but didn't indicate. Feeling sorry for her, Davey repeated his request, hoping it would remind her to indicate.

"It's OK dear, I heard you. I just don't want to go that way."

"You don't?"

"No, it'll take us back into the town. This way takes us out to a lovely view. We could have a picnic."

True, the view was lovely. Davey was hungry too. That was hardly the point though. She had to prove she could drive in traffic and perform manoeuvres and for the whole test period, not a few minutes either end of a lunch break.

"Do you like lemon drizzle? It's my speciality, but I've brought chocolate muffins too in case you don't."

"I do like lemon drizzle very much, but that's not the point, Mrs Geere."

"Of course it is." She drove to the viewing spot and parked tidily.

Davey marked her down as a pass for parallel parking.

Mrs Geere sat at a wooden picnic table, extracted a large cloth from her bag and spread it out.

Bemused, Davey joined her as she laid out cakes, quiche and two flasks.

"I bring the milk separately," she explained as though that small detail were the only thing he could possibly be wondering about.

The quiche was very good. The moist lemon drizzle with a crunchy topping was truly excellent. Davey wished he had a box to tick for that one.

Coming to his senses at last Davey said, "We have to go back now. I have another test to conduct soon."

"Yes of course, dear. And don't worry about the emergency stop. I don't like that one, especially on a full stomach. Quite shakes your insides up, doesn't it?"

"Well yes, it does, but …"

"You won't want to do that after our little picnic."

"Mrs Geere, it isn't a question of what I want." Had the food been intended as a bribe? She seemed too nice for that, but maybe after all her failures she was desperate.

"Just mark me down as not doing it, that's fair enough isn't it?"

"Well yes, but you do realise …"

"I won't pass?"

"Yes."

"Not this time no, but maybe next time. " She seemed just as amused as his colleagues had been when they'd said much the same thing an hour previously.

"Mrs Geere, I don't understand. You've taken your test a lot of times, you must want to pass, but you've not given yourself the chance."

"Why on earth would I want to pass? I don't have anywhere to keep a car and anyway travelling on the bus is much more interesting. You can look at the view and there's usually someone to talk to."

"So why take the test?"

"It's included in the price and I was brought up during the war and rationing so I don't like to waste anything."

Davey was still baffled and said so.

"After my dear husband died I thought I'd need to drive and I certainly wanted something to think about, so I booked a residential course. It was great fun, so I do it as often as I can. There are lots of people. They're usually happy to talk and always happy to eat my cakes. The courses are self catering you see. I love cooking, so I do it for everyone. Then there are the lessons. I get to go all over the place and talk to the instructor of course."

"It must be expensive."

"No more than it would be for a hotel on my own and I

don't think I'd enjoy that."

She'd driven them safely back to the test station by the time she'd explained. Davey quickly completed the paperwork, then returned to the office.

"How'd she get on, Davey, lad?"

"Very well. You know, I never expected to pass someone on their thirty-seventh attempt."

"You never passed her!"

Davey grinned. "No, but maybe next time."

Thank you for reading this book. I hope you enjoyed it. If you did, I'd really appreciate it if you could leave a short review on Amazon and/or Goodreads.

To learn more about my writing life, hear about new releases and get a free short story, sign up to my newsletter – https://mailchi.mp/677f65e1ee8f/sign-up or you can find the link on my website patsycollins.uk

More books by Patsy Collins

Novels –

Firestarter
Escape To The Country
A Year And A Day
Paint Me A Picture
Leave Nothing But Footprints
Acting Like A Killer

Non-fiction –

From Story Idea To Reader
(co-written with Rosemary J. Kind)

A Year Of Ideas:
365 sets of writing prompts and exercises

Short story collections –

Over The Garden Fence
Up The Garden Path
Through The Garden Gate
In The Garden Air

No Family Secrets
Can't Choose Your Family
Keep It In The Family
Family Feeling
Happy Families

All That Love Stuff
With Love And Kisses
Lots Of Love
Love Is The Answer

Slightly Spooky Stories I
Slightly Spooky Stories II
Slightly Spooky Stories III
Slightly Spooky Stories IV

Just A Job
A Way With Words
Dressed To Impress
Coffee & Cake
Not A Drop To Drink
Criminal Intent